JERRY MAHONEY

P9-DMT-364

My Rotten
Stepbrother Ruined
CINDERELLA

STONE ARCH BOOKS
a capstone imprint

My Rotten Stepbrother Ruined Fairy Tales is published by
Stone Arch Books, A Capstone Imprint
1710 Roe Crest Drive
North Mankato, Minnesota 56003
www.mycapstone.com

Text © 2018 Jerry Mahoney
Illustrations © 2018 Stone Arch Books

Library of Congress Cataloging-in-Publication Data
Names: Mahoney, Jerry, 1971- author. Title: My rotten stepbrother ruined
Cinderella / by Jerry Mahoney. Description: North Mankato, Minnesota :
Stone Arch Books, a Capstone imprint, [2017] | Series: My rotten stepbrother
ruined fairy tales | Summary: Maddie McMatthews is convinced that her
new stepbrother, Holden, is the worst sibling ever, especially after he ruins
her class presentation on the fairy tale Cinderella with his snide questions—
but when the two eleven-year-olds are sucked into that fairy tale, they
have to work together to restore a happy ending if they want to get home.
Identifiers: LCCN 2016036709| ISBN 9781496544667 (library binding) |
ISBN 9781496544704 (pbk.) | ISBN 9781496544827 (ebook (pdf)) Subjects:
LCSH: Cinderella (Legendary character)–Juvenile fiction. | Fairy tales. |
Magic–Juvenile fiction. | Stepbrothers–Juvenile fiction. | Brothers and
sisters–Juvenile fiction. | CYAC: Characters in literature–Fiction. | Fairy
tales–Fiction. | Magic–Fiction. | Stepbrothers–Fiction. | Brothers and sisters-
-Fiction. Classification: LCC PZ7.1.M3467 My 2017 | DDC 813.6 [Fic] –dc23
LC record available at https://lccn.loc.gov/2016036709

Illustrations: Aleksei Bitskoff

Designer: Ashlee Suker

Printed in China.
010375F17

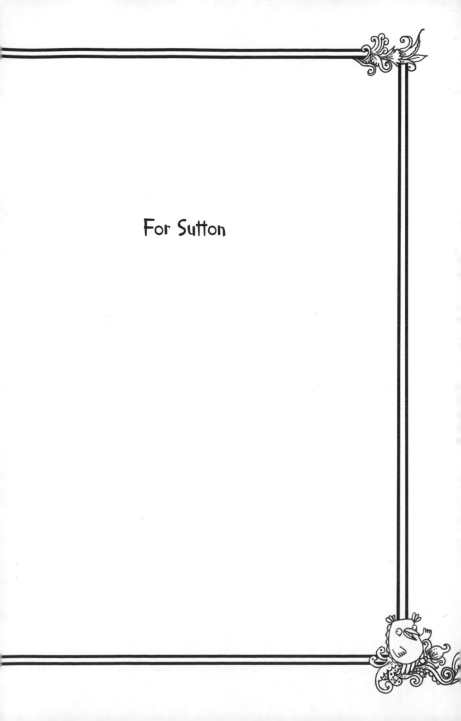

For Sutton

Chapter 1

Maddie McMatthews was pretty sure she had the worst stepbrother in the entire world. True, there might be an eleven-year-old girl in Portugal or Tajikistan whose perfectly nice stepmom had a sarcastic, prank-pulling punk for a son. Maybe that poor girl was also forced to live under the same roof as the terrible troublemaker. There was no way, though, that that girl had to put up with a boy as infuriating as Holden McNeal of Middle Grove, New Jersey. He was the obnoxious jerk with whom Maddie shared a wall, a bathroom, and a furious dislike. The two stepsiblings even shared a birthday, but Maddie was quick to correct anyone who mistakenly thought that they were twins.

"We're barely even related," she'd say with a sigh and an eye-roll.

When her dad first announced that he was marrying Carol, Maddie was thrilled. She'd always wanted a brother. She offered to show Holden around school and introduce him to everyone she knew. Then, how did he repay her? By getting them all to follow him on Instagram and posting a picture of what Maddie's hair looks like in the morning. The image got shared dozens of times and became so well-known around school that three different girls dressed as "Morning Maddie" for Halloween.

Holden became known as the class clown. She became known as the girl with clown hair.

It didn't end there. Holden erased all of Maddie's favorite shows from the DVR so he could record wrestling matches. He left his pet tarantula on her pillow so she would scream when she got into bed. None of this even came close to the worst thing he had ever done, the thing that put him in the Rotten Weasel Hall of Fame for all eternity and changed Maddie's life forever.

Her stepbrother, Holden McNeal, broke up Cinderella's wedding, forcing her to go back to scrubbing floors for her wicked stepmother.

Who even knew a fifth grader could do that?

It all started with a school assignment. Maddie had to give an oral report on her favorite story, and she chose *Cinderella*. She had always found it so beautiful and romantic, how a poor, miserable girl could fall in love with a prince and end up the most envied woman in the kingdom. Plus, lately she related to the part about having wicked stepsiblings.

As usual, Holden was determined to ruin her report the same way he ruined everything else. First he mocked her diorama, which she had spent weeks working on. It showed Cinderella walking down the aisle to marry the prince, looking stunning in a blue and white dress and her glass slippers. Maddie made tiny dolls out of old T-shirts to represent Cinderella, the prince, the wicked stepmother, and the two cruel stepsisters, who wept watching Cinderella's happily ever after.

She couldn't wait to show her family the finished work. The moment the glue dried, she carried the shoe box downstairs to present it to them in the living room. "Ta-dah!" she announced with a flourish.

Her dad and Carol were so impressed they actually started clapping.

"Maddie, you've outdone yourself," her dad cheered.

Carol gave her a giant hug. "All that hard work paid off," she gushed. "I smell an A-plus!"

But her snot of a stepbrother refused to join in the praise. He sat with his arms folded and huffed, "Why would she invite her wicked stepmother to her wedding?"

"Holden, that's not nice," Dad said to him. "It's a beautiful diorama."

"Yeah, for a lousy story."

Maddie was so hurt she responded with the meanest statement she could think of. "We'll see if I invite you to *my* wedding someday!"

Holden sneered, as he did often, and answered back with what seemed to be the meanest response he could think of. "Ugh, like I'd want to go to your wedding."

"Guys, stop it," Carol scolded.

Holden tried to act innocent. "What? I said her diorama was nice. It's just that the story was written for people who don't care if it makes sense."

"Okay, enough," Dad said. "If you two can't get along, then go to your rooms."

"Fine!"

"Fine!"

They both stormed upstairs and slammed their doors. Maddie flopped down on her bed, wanting to cry. All she had tried to do was show her parents something she was very proud of, and Holden turned it into a big fight that got them both in trouble. He was the worst!

The next day, when Mrs. Greenberg called on Maddie to do her presentation, she took a deep breath, determined not to make eye contact with her annoying stepbrother in the back row. When Maddie revealed her diorama, Mrs. Greenberg let out an impressed, "Ooh!" Maddie then gave a five-minute report on everything *Cinderella* meant to her. It was almost as if she'd been preparing this speech since she first read the story as a little girl.

"*Cinderella* is all about true love, but more than that, it's about hope. It shows that what matters most is a good heart, because as long as you have one of those, even a poor, sad servant girl can marry a prince."

She could see Mrs. Greenberg nodding approvingly, and Maddie couldn't help glaring at Holden in the back row. "Not to mention," she added, "she can also triumph over her wicked stepsiblings."

She knew Holden would figure out this was directed

at him, but what she didn't expect was that the entire class would break out laughing and turn to face him.

"Quiet down, everyone," Mrs. Greenberg said. Maddie felt a little bad for Holden, but it served him right for criticizing her diorama. Then as Maddie gathered her notes to go back to her seat, Mrs. Greenberg turned to the classroom and said the words every student dreads. "Any questions?"

There's an unwritten rule among students that question time will always be met with silence. No one wants to ask questions after anyone else's report, because no one wants to have to answer questions after their own report.

Maddie picked up her diorama to return to her seat, when out of the corner of her eye, she saw a hand go up in the back of the room.

"I have some questions," a very familiar, very snotty voice said.

Maddie turned to see her stepbrother, Holden, shooting that same smug grin back at her. She had a strong urge to hurl her diorama directly at his head.

"Yes, Holden?" Mrs. Greenberg said. "Go ahead."

Holden took a deep breath. Clearly, he'd been preparing for this. "First of all, if the prince was so in love with

Cinderella, why would he have to identify her by her foot? Wouldn't he remember her face?"

Maddie sighed. He thought he was so smart. "Actually, fairy tales are full of mistaken identity," she said. "Little Red Riding Hood even mistook a wolf for her grandmother. So it makes sense that the prince wouldn't trust his memory."

Mrs. Greenberg nodded again. It was a solid answer. Maddie hoped that would get Holden to back off, but instead, he tilted his questioning head to the other side and launched another attack. "Tell me something," he said, loudly. "What shoe size do you wear?"

"Me?" Maddie asked.

"Yes. I'm curious."

Maddie shook her head. What could the rotten monster be up to now? "I'm a five and a half."

"Thanks. Just out of curiosity, is anyone else here a five and a half?" He looked around the room. "C'mon, raise your hands if you wear a size five and a half."

A few hands shot up. "One, two, three, four, five . . . ," Holden counted. "So, Maddie, you have the same size foot as about half the girls in this class. Let me ask you, do you think shoe size is a reliable way to identify someone?"

"That's not fair!"

"Isn't it? What if the glass slipper had happened to fit another woman before the prince even got to Cinderella? He might've married the wrong person."

Maddie groaned. She wanted to shut him down, but to her horror, Mrs. Greenberg was nodding her head at him now. Was she actually agreeing with that little creep?

"One more thing," Holden said. "How did Cinderella get home from the ball?"

Maddie smirked. He thought he was so clever that he could make her fall for a trick question like this. If she didn't know the story so well, she might've said that Cinderella rode home in her coach, but of course, that wouldn't have been possible.

"Well, her coach changed back into a pumpkin at the stroke of midnight," Maddie replied. "So obviously she walked." Nice try, Holden.

Satisfied that she had answered the question correctly, Maddie began to gather her things so she could sit back down at last.

Unfortunately, Holden wasn't finished.

"With one shoe?" he asked.

"Why not?"

"Wasn't this before roads were paved? Weren't villages many miles away from the palace? That must've been agony."

"It was," Maddie said, feeling much like Cinderella at that moment. "It was absolute agony."

"Well, it's a lovely story," Mrs. Greenberg said. "Even if it is flawed."

Maddie flopped back down into her seat. Flawed? How could anyone think that *Cinderella* was flawed? She was furious with Holden for ruining her report.

What she didn't realize yet was that her stepbrother had ruined a lot more than that.

Chapter
2

Maddie stayed up late that night wondering how to get her dad to divorce Carol.

She imagined how good it would feel to see Holden packing all his Star Wars and Avengers figures into boxes and rounding up all his video games. She'd even help him load the truck and cheerily wave goodbye as he pulled away forever. As comforting as the thought was, though, she couldn't help but feel bad for her father. He'd been so much happier since he met Carol. Maddie had to admit she was a really nice woman, even if she had raised a troll for a son.

Once Maddie had ruled out the thought of breaking up her father's marriage, she comforted herself by calculating the exact number of days between now and when she and Holden both left for college. As good as she was at math, multiplying by 365 was exhausting, and that's how she finally fell asleep.

It wasn't much later that there was a soft but urgent knock on her bedroom door. At first the knock didn't wake her, but then came another, louder knock. And another, even louder one. Maddie rolled over groggily and looked at her clock. She couldn't figure out why someone would possibly be bothering her at 12:04 a.m. As for who was doing it, that was a much easier question to answer.

"Holden, go away. It's, like, a million o'clock."

"Open your door, Maddie," Holden demanded from the hallway. "This isn't funny."

There was no way Maddie was going to open the door. She was convinced he was planning some cruel trick that could only be pulled off in the middle of the night. "Go back to bed, Holden. I'm not opening my —"

Maddie stopped short as something across the room caught her eye. The thin slivers of light that fell through her blinds shined on her diorama, and something about it looked very different. Not believing her eyes, Maddie rose from her bed to examine it. Sure enough, the dolls had been moved around to depict a completely different scene. Now, one of the wicked stepsisters was marrying the prince, and Cinderella was sitting in the corner, crying. Was this Holden's gag? Had he somehow snuck into her room and messed with her project? Furious, she thrust open her bedroom door and shoved the shoe box in his face.

"What did you do to my diorama?" she demanded.

He didn't hear her say it, though, because at exactly the same moment, he said just as loudly, "What did you do to my tablet?"

Then at the same time, they said, "What did you say?"

"Look at my diorama! It's all messed up!" Maddie accused.

"I didn't touch it," Holden insisted. "I was asleep until you made my tablet turn on."

"What are you talking about?" Maddie asked. "I haven't touched your tablet."

"Wait a second . . . ," Holden said, taking a closer look at Maddie's diorama. "I don't believe it. Maddie, you have to see this."

"See what?"

Holden grabbed her by the arm. "Come on." He pulled her down the hallway toward his room.

"Holden, if this is a trick, I'm going to wake up my dad, and you'll be in so much trouble."

"Look," he told her, pushing open the door to his room.

It was the usual disaster area it always was, where every surface was covered with Oreo crumbs, dirty socks, and the cars section of the newspaper. One thing stood out, though, in the midnight darkness. On top of Holden's desk, his tablet computer was emitting a soft, eerie glow.

"You shouldn't leave your screen on," Maddie said. "It wastes battery power."

"I can't turn it off," Holden said. "Go look at it."

Maddie kicked aside debris to clear a path to the desk, then gazed down curiously at the illuminated screen. On it was a beautifully ornate title page for an e-book. In tall, scripted letters was a name she knew quite well. *Cinderella*, it read.

Maddie groaned. "I knew this was a trick. Did you really have to wake me up in the middle of the night to start the *Cinderella* fight all over again?"

"I swear," Holden said. "I woke up and saw this. I didn't do anything. Now flip to the end."

With a sigh, Maddie swiped her finger across the screen. She saw beautiful drawings of Cinderella scrubbing her stepmother's floor, meeting with her fairy godmother, and arriving at the ball in her pumpkin coach. Then there was a picture that didn't make sense. Cinderella was walking home from the ball with no shoes on, holding her swollen foot in pain.

"It's like I said," Holden explained. "She had to walk home with no shoes on, so look at her foot. It's all bruised."

"But that's not part of the story," Maddie said. She stared at the drawing, confused. There was no way Holden could have made this picture himself. Any time he tried to draw a person, it ended up looking like a lopsided cow. This was a beautiful illustration, of a scene that didn't exist in any version of Cinderella Maddie had ever read. If he didn't draw it, then how did it get in there?

The e-book only got stranger after that. There was a picture of the prince trying the glass slipper on one of Cinderella's wicked stepsisters, then one of him kissing her. The prince kissing a stepsister? No way.

"This is so weird," Maddie said.

"Just wait," Holden said. "Check out the last page."

Maddie flipped to the end and saw a detailed sketch of the prince marrying the wicked stepsister, while Cinderella sat alone in a corner, crying.

"No, it can't be . . . ," Maddie said. She held her diorama next to the tablet and looked back and forth between the two. The similarities were astounding. The dresses the characters wore, the expressions on their faces, the flowers in the bouquet. The two scenes were virtually identical. "How did you do that?" she asked Holden.

"I'm telling you, I didn't," he said. "You know I can't draw, and I haven't been in your room all night. I think . . . I think we broke *Cinderella*."

"What do you mean? You can't break a story. *Cinderella*'s been around for hundreds of years."

"You have another copy of it, right?" Holden said. "Go get it."

Maddie rolled her eyes. "Fine. But then I'm going back to bed."

Maddie walked back to her room to get her copy of *Cinderella*, as Holden paced nervously.

"It must've been those questions I asked," he said to himself. "The stepsister had the same size foot as Cinderella, so the shoe fit her, and then she married the prince. The prince didn't realize his mistake because he couldn't remember Cinderella's face. Of course!"

"Here it is," Maddie said, entering with a hardbound picture book of *Cinderella*. It was old and tattered and well-loved, as books should be. "This is the copy my dad has been reading to me since I was a little girl, with a fairy godmother and a ball and a happily ever —"

Maddie flipped to the last page of the book, but as she saw the picture there, she dropped the book in shock. "No! It's not possible! How —?"

Holden picked the book up and looked at the last page. Just like in the diorama and the e-book, the illustration showed Cinderella's stepsister marrying the prince. Instead of "Happily Ever After," it said simply, "The End."

Maddie glared at her stepbrother. "I can't believe you broke my favorite story!"

"What do we do?"

"Gimme the book!" Maddie said, grabbing it from him. "I'm reading it from the beginning to see how much you messed it up."

Holden picked up his tablet and swiped through the pages. "I had no idea I had this power," he said proudly. "I wonder what else I could break. Maybe I could write some ninjas into *The Secret Garden*, so it wouldn't be so boring."

Maddie flipped back to the first page of *Cinderella* and began to read. "Once upon a time . . . "

Before Maddie could continue, she felt a weird tingling sensation. "What's going on?" she asked. Holden began to feel it too.

A huge flash of light rose out of the tablet, enveloping Maddie and Holden. To Maddie's amazement, her body began to shrink and float across the room. Slowly, she could see herself getting sucked into the tablet.

"Maddie!" Holden shouted. He held out his hand to save her, but it was no use. He was getting pulled in too.

At the same moment, the tablet and the book both fell to the floor. The two stepsiblings sank together into the pages, and the cover illustration on each copy changed. Instead of Cinderella in a pumpkin coach, it now showed Holden and Maddie, gazing around a fairy tale world and looking incredibly confused.

It was the only trace of them left in the bedroom.

Chapter
3

The next thing Maddie and Holden knew, they were absolutely nowhere. There was no other way to describe where they were, really, because there was nothing at all to describe. There was nothing behind or in front of them, nothing above or below. No buildings, no people, not even a drop of color. They were just two fifth graders looking at pure, plain whiteness in every direction, and it was freaky. They couldn't be sure if they were indoors or outdoors, on the ground or thousands of feet in the sky.

Holden turned to Maddie and shrugged, as if to ask, "What is this crazy place?"

Maddie wanted to respond, but she couldn't think of anything to say. Her mind was totally blank, until suddenly, she shouted, "Duck!"

She pointed at a large, black, stringy object, the first thing she had seen in wherever it was they were. It came at them fast, flying directly toward Holden's head.

Holden might not have had much to say, but when he heard the word *duck*, he ducked, just in time to avoid the flying object. "What was that?" he said.

As Maddie breathed a sigh of relief, Holden yelled out, "Maddie!" and grabbed her by the arm. He yanked her out of the way as a similar object whizzed past her.

Then came another strange, dark doodad. And another. The two stepsiblings leapt back and forth to dodge them, and soon they were able to figure out exactly what the mysterious objects were.

"They're words," Maddie declared. Then something even stranger started to happen. With each word that flew by, the plain white world in which they stood began to fill with color and life.

Maddie saw the word *forest*, and then behind her appeared lush green woods, full of trees and babbling, winding brooks.

Holden observed the word *mice* as it magically transformed into a half-dozen squealing, red-nosed rodents.

Then came the word *cottage*, and the two stepsiblings watched as a picturesque house appeared atop a hill in the distance.

Neither of them was at a loss for what to say anymore. Instead, they called out every word that appeared, just before it transformed into whatever it said.

"Hedgehog!" Maddie read, and then a hedgehog dropped at her feet. It quickly balled up and rolled away from her into the woods.

She watched it go until Holden let out a stunned "Whoa!" She turned for a glimpse of what had left him in such awe, and there she saw the most amazing sight of her life. Before her eyes, the word *castle* transformed into an epically large, majestic palace, with turrets and spires and the flag of an unknown kingdom flying overhead.

It was then that Maddie realized where she now stood: in a magical fairy tale kingdom straight out of a storybook. The world was filling in around them as if it were being written in that moment.

The next word she saw read *foot soldier*. She looked around for the foot soldier, but she couldn't see one. "Holden," she said, "do you see—" She stopped short as she turned toward her stepbrother. Before her eyes, the boy who tormented her day and night transformed into a royal guard in full uniform, with a sword by his side.

"What's wrong, Maddie?" he asked.

"You're a foot soldier!"

Before he could respond, more words came toward them, hurtling faster and faster.

"Flowers!"

"Ballroom!"

"Wedding!"

The next word wasn't a word at all. *Glamoremma*, it read. What was that? Maddie looked back at Holden, but he was no longer there. And she was no longer in an empty world watching words fly by. She was now sitting at a table in a beautiful ballroom with her hands on the most exquisite crystal vase she had ever seen.

She had been transported inside the castle.

She'd seen a thousand castles in a thousand storybooks, but nothing prepared her for the feeling of being in one. The gold and the gems were so pure she felt like she'd need sunglasses to look directly at them. The marble floors were so shiny they reflected everything above them, as if an exact copy of the room stretched out upside-down below her feet. The ceiling was so high Maddie wouldn't have been surprised to see a flock of geese migrating over her head.

Everything was spectacular, and Maddie was suddenly overcome with the irresistible urge to burst into song. The excitement swelled inside her as majestic chords began to play in her head. She took a deep breath, opened her mouth wide, and. . . .

Thankfully, though, she stopped herself before she sang a note. That probably would've been a little weird.

Besides, everyone around her seemed terribly busy preparing for a special occasion. They were hanging garlands and setting tables with precious china. Everyone she saw was dressed immaculately in bright, tailored clothes. Every man wore a freshly pressed uniform, and every woman wore an elegant dress.

Maddie caught the attention of a housemaid passing by. "Excuse me," she said. "Could you tell me what everyone's preparing for?"

"Why, the royal wedding, My Lady," the housemaid replied, before scurrying off with an armful of tablecloths.

"Lady?" Maddie had never been called a lady before. She looked down at what she was wearing, and to her surprise, she *was* a lady. From her neck to her feet stretched the most dazzling gown she had ever seen. It was pink and white and covered in glitter. Maddie thought it would make a killer prom dress someday.

Then a final word flew overhead, a word that couldn't have seemed more out of place amid all the cheer and excitement around the room.

"Tears."

The word settled above the head of a young woman a few feet away from Maddie, and as it did, the woman began to weep. Maddie hadn't seen her before, but she could tell that this woman had plenty to be sad about, starting with her clothes. They were filthy, patched-up work clothes, and her hair was tied back with a rag. She sat in front of a pile of roses, and one by one, she plucked the thorns off each stem and placed them into a vase. Her hands were scratched and bruised from hours of performing this tedious, excruciating task. No wonder she was crying.

"Do you need a tissue?" Maddie asked her.

"Tissue?" the woman replied. "What's a tissue?" The woman turned her head and gazed up at Maddie, confused.

Of course, Maddie thought. *They don't have tissues in fairy tales. They weren't invented yet.* While she wondered how to explain this, she had another realization. This wasn't any ordinary, sad woman. She was kind and familiar, the most beautiful woman Maddie had ever seen. She had bright blue eyes and, underneath the rag on her head, hair that seemed to be made from pure gold.

"Oh my gosh!" Maddie exclaimed. "You're — you're Cinderella!"

"You seem surprised to see me, Glamoremma," the young woman replied.

Chapter 4

"Glamoremma?" Maddie repeated uncertainly. It was that strange word that had flown past her earlier. Was it a name? Was it *her* name? She stared at the stunning woman beside her and realized something even stranger: when Maddie called this woman Cinderella, the woman didn't correct her. That meant Maddie was right. She was standing in a palace talking to the one and only Cinderella.

"Didn't you know your mother was having me prepare for your sister's wedding?" Cinderella continued.

"My sister?" Maddie said. "You mean I'm —?" She looked down at her dress again. It was so beautiful and clean, the opposite of Cinderella's ragged work clothes. Of course. With a name like Glamoremma, it was clear who she'd become in this story. She was a wicked stepsister.

"I just want this wedding to be over so I can go back to working in Stepmother's house," Cinderella sniffled. "At least there, no one will see me cry."

"So it's true? The prince is marrying one of the wicked step —, I mean, the prince is marrying my sister?"

"Why do you delight in hearing me say it?" Cinderella asked. "You were there when she tried the glass slipper on. It was a perfect fit. My swollen feet were far too big." She nodded toward her feet, which were red and bruised.

Maddie's jaw dropped. "Yes, because you walked home from the ball, just like Holden said."

"Holden?" Cinderella repeated, confused.

"Oh no," Maddie said. She pushed her chair back from the table to stand up. "This is not how it's supposed to be. This is all my fault. Well, don't worry. I'm going to do my best to fix everyth — WHAAA!"

She hadn't intended to say "WHAAA!" of course, but that's the kind of thing that comes out of your mouth when you realize you're about to fall flat on your face. No sooner had Maddie stood up than she lost her balance. She tried to grab hold of something to keep herself from collapsing, but in her panic, she chose to reach for the vase, and there has yet to be a vase made that could hold the weight of an eleven-year-old girl. The instant Maddie's hand brushed against it, the vase began to roll toward the opposite edge of the table. Now she knew she was going down, and she was going down hard. As she fell, she noticed why she hadn't been able to stand up in the first place. On her feet were six-inch high-heel shoes.

The only time Maddie had worn high heels before was when she'd dressed as Cinderella three Halloweens ago. Even then, she only made it about half a block because the heels were impossible to walk in. After that, she made a mental note to choose only Halloween costumes that included sensible shoes.

"URRRFF!" was the sound that Maddie made as she hit the floor. Thankfully, nobody heard her because at the exact same moment she was URRRFF-ing in pain, the crystal vase was rolling off the table.

If you've ever heard glass shatter, you know how attention-getting the sound can be. When the glass is a priceless crystal vase, the shattering sound isn't any louder, but it does draw quite a bit more attention.

Every single eye in the ballroom focused on Maddie, Cinderella, and the obliterated vase. The entire castle seemed to fall totally silent, but only for a moment. Then, a deep, sinister voice rose up from across the room.

"HOWWWW DAAAAARE YOOOOOU!" the voice bellowed.

A woman stood up. She was not a large woman, yet she cast a towering shadow that stretched all the way across the room and fell directly on Cinderella. The temperature seemed to fall ten degrees in that instant, and everyone shuddered as this fuming giant strutted grimly toward the downhearted woman.

Clunk, clunk, clunk. The floor seemed to shake with her every footstep. Everyone she passed turned to avoid her gaze. A few were heard to whisper in frightened tones, "Pernicia!"

As the woman approached them, Maddie saw the most fearsome face she had ever laid eyes on. The furious woman had a high forehead with jagged black and gray hair that spilled over her ears in waves. Her eyes were sharp like daggers, able to cut you with merely a glance in your direction, every lash perfectly straight like a needle. When she scowled, all her wrinkles disappeared, which seemed to indicate that this was the expression with which her face was most comfortable. If the woman next to Maddie was Cinderella, there was no doubt who was bearing down on them so fiercely.

"You're trying to ruin this wedding!" the wicked stepmother thundered.

"No!" Maddie gasped, too intimidated to speak above a whisper. "It was an accident!"

"Step aside, Glamoremma," the stepmother said, edging Maddie over with the back of her hand. "This is between me and your stepsister."

The pitiless woman bent over Cinderella, who winced as if to prepare for a blistering punishment. "You've been upset ever since the prince proposed to your stepsister. But I won't let you ruin her wedding."

"Stepmother," Cinderella pleaded. "I would never do anything to ruin Prince Andrew's wedding."

"You're right, you won't, because you'll spend the next few days in the dungeon."

"Stepmother, no! Please!" Cinderella begged.

"Foot soldier!" the stepmother shouted.

Foot soldier? Maddie thought. *Could it be –?*

With a mighty whoosh, the doors to the ballroom thrust open, and a royal foot soldier marched across the floor in their direction. As he came into view, Maddie breathed a sigh of relief.

It was Holden, dressed in a guard's uniform.

"So yeah, like, what's up?" Holden said as he approached the wicked stepmother.

Maddie grabbed him by the shoulders. She had never been so happy to see her stepbrother. "Holden! It's me," she told him.

"Maddie?" he asked, now recognizing her. To everyone else, she looked like a grown-up, but he could see her for who she really was, the eleven-year-old girl who always hogged the bathroom in the morning before school.

The wicked stepmother stepped in between them. "Maddie?" she said. "No, this is my beloved daughter, Glamoremma."

On hearing her name, Holden burst out laughing. "*Glamoremma*? What a nutty name."

"I beg your pardon," the stepmother said. "Her sister is about to become your princess, and I shall be the mistress of this castle."

"Geez," Holden said, turning to Maddie. "What's up with her?"

"That's Cinderella's stepmother," Maddie explained with a nudge.

"Pernicia V. Rockbotton to you," the stepmother said. "I order you to lock this treacherous wench in the dungeon for trying to ruin the royal wedding."

"Well, he won't do it," Maddie said. She smiled at her stepbrother, glad to have someone on her side.

"He'll do as I say!" thundered Pernicia. "Take Cinderella to the dungeon at once!"

"Hang on," Holden said. "This is Cinderella?"

"That is what they call me," Cinderella said.

Holden laughed again. "Awesome! Somebody tell me where the dungeon is." He grabbed Cinderella by the arm and lifted her to her feet.

Pernicia pointed across the room. "Head down those stairs until the light of hope is all but gone and the stench of misery is overwhelming."

"Got it," Holden replied.

"Holden, no!" Maddie pleaded.

"Sorry," Holden said. "I'm a foot soldier, and an order's an order."

Maddie watched in disbelief as her stepbrother led Cinderella out of the ballroom. He was enjoying this, the little worm. She was going to have to stop him. Cinderella would never be able to marry the prince if she was locked in a dungeon.

"Glamoremma," Pernicia hissed as she turned back to Maddie, "I thought I taught you better than to have pity on that sad little servant girl." Pernicia shook her head disapprovingly, then clomped back across the room.

"Sorry, Mother," Maddie responded. She watched until the wicked stepmother was out of sight, then she kicked off her heels and scurried after her stepbrother and Cinderella.

Chapter 5

The winding stairs that led to the dungeon were steep, narrow, and seemed to go on forever. They also produced a loud echo, so as Maddie descended, she was able to hear everything Holden was saying to his prisoner.

"So you're Cinderella?" he asked.

"Have you heard of me?" Cinderella replied.

"Well, yeah. You're kind of famous. You live with your stepmother. She won't let you go to the ball. Then your fairy godmother comes and, shazam, you're all fancy."

Cinderella gasped. "How did you know about my fairy godmother?"

"Duh. It's part of the story. Then you marry the prince and live happily ever after."

"I only wish. I've never felt such love as I did with him, but I'm afraid he's preparing to marry my stepsister."

"Oh, right," Holden said. "Stinks to be you."

Maddie was having a hard time keeping up with them

barefoot. *No wonder Cinderella's feet had suffered so much on the walk home,* she thought. Holden, the sneak that he was, had actually made kind of a good point.

Finally, she reached the bottom of the staircase. There, she found herself in a dim, musty room, where green ooze dripped from every crack in the walls. As she stepped into the doorway, Maddie was assaulted by the most horrible odor she had ever gotten a whiff of.

Apparently, Holden smelled it too. "Yuck," he said. "It smells like old cheese and gym socks down here."

Out of the shadows stepped a large, bearded man wearing an armored breastplate and carrying a spear. "Who goes there?" he barked.

"This is Cinderella," Holden said, holding his nose. "Who are you?"

"I am the dungeon master," the man said. "I shall take her from here."

Maddie stopped short when she saw the fearsome dungeon master. She hid in the doorway, a safe distance from him.

"Great," Holden said. "So I can get out of this stink hole?" He handed Cinderella off to the dungeon master.

"Later, Cinderella," he called, as he marched back toward the stairs.

"Come with me," the dungeon master told the frightened woman. "To the deepest, darkest cell you shall go."

Holden stopped and turned around. "Hang on," he said. "Does it have to be the deepest, darkest cell? I mean, she seems nice."

Maddie couldn't believe it. Was her stepbrother feeling a tiny bit guilty?

The dungeon master scoffed. "She shall share a cell with the vilest criminal known to our kingdom, Darreth, Duke of the Darkness." *BOOM!* As soon as the dungeon master uttered the name, a mighty clap of thunder shook the walls of the dungeon.

"What was that?" Holden asked.

"His name is so feared," the dungeon master said, "that the gods spit great walls of thunder every time they hear it."

"Really?" Holden said. "So if I say Darreth, Duke of the Dark —?" *BOOM!* Another wave of thunder roared through the cold stone room. "That's awesome cool!" He couldn't help smiling, until he saw the fear on Cinderella's face. "I mean, I'm sure he's not that bad."

"Not bad?" the dungeon master exclaimed. "He invaded our kingdom and brought a wave of disease and hardship never before known in our land. You know of him, right, prisoner?"

Cinderella bowed her head and took a deep breath. "Of course," she whispered. "Prince Andrew nearly died defeating him. After the battle, he decided he should settle down and marry so he could produce an heir. That's why he threw the ball. Everyone's heard of Darreth, Duke of the Darkness."

BOOM! Another massive thunder clap sounded.

The dungeon master led Cinderella toward a cell where an enormous, sinister shadow lurked. Just looking at his silhouette gave Holden the shivers. "Okay, if you don't need me, I'll be heading out," he said, backing away.

Holden turned to go upstairs, only to find himself face-to-face with Maddie. She was angrier than he had ever seen her. "How could you, Holden?" she exploded. "This is the meanest thing you've ever done."

"Look, if you want to make me feel guilty about locking Cinderella in a dungeon, save your breath," he said, "because I already do."

"Then get her out of there. You know she's supposed to marry the prince, and she can't do it when she's down here."

"Fine, fine. Um, excuse me? Dungeon master?" Holden turned around, and the dungeon master stepped out from the shadows, Cinderella quivering at his side.

"What is it?" he demanded, annoyed.

"Look, the woman you're locking up, she's not so bad," Holden explained. "She kind of got a raw deal. So maybe we should let her out, give her another chance."

Cinderella smiled hopefully and gazed up at the massive dungeon master to see if he, too, had had a change of heart.

The dungeon master spat on the floor. "Once a prisoner is delivered to me, she can only be freed by decree of the prince himself!" He turned around and marched with Cinderella back into the cold, gloomy darkness of the dungeon.

Holden looked at Maddie and shrugged. "I tried."

Chapter 6

Maddie wasn't sure what to yell at Holden first. "I hate you!" came to mind, as did "I super mega hate you!" and "Arrrrrrrgh, why are you so horrible?" She decided to wait until she got to the top of the stairs before unleashing her insult, so she'd have time to think of something mean enough for what he deserved. By then, she'd crafted a brilliant zinger, using some of the biggest words she could think of: "The depth of your weenieness stupefies me." Yes, it was perfect. She steered him into a quiet hallway, took a deep breath, and prepared to wallop him with it, when he turned toward her with a big, goofy grin on his face.

"Wow, you're in your favorite story," he said. "This must be really cool for you."

In an instant, Maddie forgot what she was going to say, and all that came out was a muffled, furious yelp. If she hadn't had so much self-control, she would've screamed loud enough to shake the castle to the ground.

"You locked Cinderella in a dungeon," she seethed. "This is not cool."

"Well, if you're not having fun either," he said, "then let's go home."

Maddie scoffed. "Oh, sure. And I'm guessing you have a map that leads back to reality?"

"Well, I have this," he shrugged. Holden reached into the coat of his uniform and pulled out his tablet.

"What?" Maddie grabbed the tablet and checked around to make sure no one saw it. "You can't have that. Fairy tales don't have tablets."

"This one does," he said. "It's what got us here, and maybe it can get us home."

He took the tablet back from her.

"I don't believe this," Maddie groaned. "What could you find on your tablet that could possibly help us here?"

"How about this?" Holden said.

Maddie took one look at the screen and her jaw dropped. What she saw was an illustration from the *Cinderella* e-book, one that hadn't been there earlier. In it, the dungeon master was locking Cinderella in a cell. "That's exactly what just happened!" Maddie gasped.

"Yeah, except for those two weirdos," Holden replied. He pointed to two figures in the background of the drawing, who were watching as Cinderella got locked up.

"Holden, those weirdos are us," Maddie informed him.

"Huh?"

"Really. Look at this."

Maddie held up the tablet and turned on the camera. "What are you doing?" Holden asked.

"I'm taking a selfie." Maddie reversed the camera onto the two of them, but instead of two eleven-year-olds, the image showed two grown-ups — a stern, balding foot soldier and a mean, scowling stepsister.

"Whoa!" Holden said. "That is us!"

"That's how the characters in the story see us. You're a foot soldier to the prince and I'm a wicked stepsister named Glamoremma."

Holden wasn't paying attention to her anymore. He was using the tablet to take pictures of the top of his head. "Is this what I'm going to look like as a grown-up? Am I going to go bald?"

Maddie grabbed the tablet away from him. "Stop looking at your bald spot, Holden. What matters now is what happens next in the story." She swiped her finger across the screen to pull up the next page, but all she got was an error message. *Error: Happily Ever After unavailable.*

"Rats," Holden said. "I guess we'll never know."

"Of course we will," Maddie said. "Don't you get it? We'll know what happens when we *make* it happen."

"What are you talking about?"

"We broke the story, so now we have to fix it. We can't go home until we give Cinderella back her happily ever after."

"How do we do that?" he asked.

"Well, we know we can change the story."

"Right! Because I got Cinderella locked in the dungeon."

"Right," Maddie said, gritting her teeth. "Now we have to change it the right way."

Holden tucked the tablet back inside his coat. "Okay, I'm a royal guardsman, so why don't I just tell the prince he's marrying the wrong woman and that the real love of his life is locked in a dungeon? Done."

"He'll think you're nuts. Besides, this is a fairy tale. We have to do something fairy tale-ish."

"Ooh!" Holden snapped his fingers excitedly. He looked like he wanted to high-five himself. "I'll turn myself into a fire-breathing dragon, then kidnap Cinderella and take her to my mountain lair. Then the prince will have to come slay me so he can save her, and that's when they'll fall in love."

"Holden —"

"Let's try it. Shazam!" Holden waved his hands in the air, twirled around, and snapped his fingers, but nothing happened. When he stopped spinning, he staggered dizzily on his feet. "Am I a dragon?"

"Nope."

"Hmmm . . . what about . . . hocus pocus! Ziggity-yow-yow!" He tried waving his hands some more, but still, he remained completely un-dragon-like.

"I don't think the magic words are the problem, Holden. You're a foot soldier, not a sorcerer. Besides, do you really want the prince to slay you?"

"I guess not," he sighed. "But breathing fire would've been sweet."

"We have to come up with a plan we can actually do."

"Do you have any ideas?"

"No. I guess we'll have to wait until an idea hits us."

No sooner had the words come out of Maddie's mouth than a large crystal goblet came flying at her head.

"Maddie, look out!" Holden shouted. He grabbed her and pulled her aside, and she barely avoided the shattering glass as it smashed against the wall, inches from her head.

"Whoa!" she said, catching her breath. "Thanks, Holden. You saved me from — um, what are you doing?"

Holden once again had his faced buried in the tablet. "I'm waiting to see if that shows up in the book," he said. "That was so cool!"

From inside the room, Maddie could hear more glass smashing. Clearly, whatever had happened was not an accident. Someone was throwing things all over the place. Maddie tiptoed toward the doorway, motioning for Holden to get behind her. "We'd better check this out."

Chapter
7

Holden and Maddie peeked nervously into the room the goblet had come flying out of. From the commotion, they half expected to see a hurricane or a Godzilla wreaking havoc inside. Instead, it was a petite woman in a wedding dress and a ton of makeup who was destroying everything she could get her hands on. There were glass shards everywhere. Torn fabric and splattered food too. Three royal staffers took shelter underneath a table in hopes this rampaging screwball might eventually settle down.

Finally, a butler reached up his quivering hand. He very skittishly placed a goblet on the table in front of the woman. "W-w-we were thinking of these glasses, Your Grace, for the royal t-t-toast."

As soon as he set it down, the woman snatched it up and hurled it against the wall.

"I HATE IT! I HATE IT! I HATE IT!" she shouted as slivers of glass rained down.

Holden and Maddie ducked back into the hallway, overwhelmed by the scene.

"Whoa, she's nuts," Holden whispered. "They should call security."

"Um, you're security," Maddie replied, motioning toward his guard's uniform.

"Oh, right. Well, I'm not going anywhere near her."

Back inside the room, the staffers were trying their best to calm the woman. "What is it you want, My Lady?" a housemaid asked. "We'll get you anything!"

"I just want to stop! Picking! Glasses!" the woman wailed. *SMASH! SMASH!* She waved her arm across the table, sending every priceless piece of crystal crashing to the floor.

Out in the hallway, Maddie whispered to Holden. "I bet that's the other stepsister."

"She's definitely wicked," Holden agreed. "I wonder what her name is. Loonylily? Smashysally?"

The butler tried to reason with the hostile woman. "B-but these decisions must be made before the w-wedding, Beautianna."

"HAHAHAHA!" As soon as he heard the name, Holden burst out laughing. "That's the wackiest name yet!"

he said. It was only then that he realized that everyone had heard him — the housemaid, the butler, and, unfortunately, even the wicked stepsister with the wacky name. She turned angrily toward the doorway and seethed at him, ready to do to Holden what she'd been doing to the glasses.

Maddie backed away. She always secretly enjoyed when her stepbrother got in trouble. It was fun to watch him squirm for a change, the little rat.

He definitely had it coming.

Beautianna stomped across the room toward Holden. As she approached, he held up his hands to shield his face. "Please don't throw anything at me!"

"Who are you?" she demanded. "Don't you know I can have you executed?"

"Ex-ex-executed?" Holden stammered.

Maddie gasped. As much as she wanted to see Holden punished, she didn't think he quite deserved to get his head chopped off in a guillotine. Besides, a scene like that would *really* ruin Cinderella.

Summoning all her courage, Maddie leaped in front of her stepbrother. "He didn't mean it," she said. "Please don't hurt him."

Beautianna turned toward Maddie, and Maddie feared what she might do next. Maybe she'd have them both executed. Maddie braced herself for the worst.

Then Beautianna spread out her arms and threw them around Maddie in a warm, tight hug.

"Sissy!" Beautianna squealed.

In an instant, the raging woman softened. It was clear this wicked stepsister hated picking out wedding china, but it was just as clear that she loved her sister.

"Oh, how I've missed you today! You wouldn't believe what these palace nitwits have been making me do. Pick out decorations, pose for portraits, stand for hours to get this awful dress fitted."

At last, she released Maddie from the hug, then became instantly grumpy again as she turned toward Holden. "Is this man bothering you, Sissy?"

Maddie smiled. All Holden had ever done was bother her. She could get him in so much trouble right now. Maybe he'd get thrown in the dungeon just like Cinderella.

"No, he's okay," Maddie said. As much as she wanted him gone, he was the only other person here who could help her fix this story.

Beautianna smiled and whispered in Maddie's ear. "Well, he's quite handsome. Do you fancy him?"

"No! Yuck!" Maddie said.

Beautianna giggled. "Well, if my sissy likes you, then you can stay. The rest of you, be gone. Leave us!"

The staff members cautiously came out from underneath the table where they'd been hiding.

"Your Grace," the handmaid said, "we need to finalize the wedding plans today."

"Get out!" Beautianna screamed.

As quickly as they could, the three staffers scurried into the hallway.

"Come on in, Sissy. Today has been agony!"

Beautianna sat down on the one chair that wasn't covered in broken glass.

"Why are you so upset, um, Sissy?" Maddie asked. "You're marrying the prince."

"I know. In a hideous dress I hate," Beautianna whimpered. She grabbed her sleeve and yanked it as hard as she could, tearing a huge rip across the shoulder.

"No!" Maddie gasped. "It's gorgeous. I would love to get married in a dress like that."

"I'm with Beautianna," Holden said. "Why do wedding dresses always have to be white? You can't have any fun. You have to stay out of the mud. You have to worry about spilling stuff on them. If I ever get married, my wife will wear a bathing suit, and we'll have a pool wedding."

Beautianna glared at Holden like he was insane. "You're sure he's all right?" she asked Maddie.

"Believe it or not, he is," Maddie said. "So if you don't like that dress, what do you want to wear?"

"I'll show you!" Beautianna chirped happily. "I designed it myself."

"Great," Maddie replied. "If you designed it yourself, it must be —"

Before she could finish her thought, Beautianna handed her a sketch. It was a very elaborate design of what was probably the absolute last dress Maddie could imagine a woman ever wanting to get married in. It was bursting with color, rainbow-striped, and covered with sequins, with giant peacock feathers jutting out of the back and on top of the veil. It looked like something Katy Perry might wear in concert, with her hair dyed pink and backup dancers dressed like leprechauns.

"Whoa, now that's rad," Holden said. "Can I use that design on my skateboard?"

"But that's not a wedding dress," Maddie disagreed. "And it's not very princess-like. The royal family could never let you get married in that."

"I don't like asking permission for what I can wear," Beautianna pouted. "Everything I do is wrong around here. I don't dress right, I don't act right. I'm the worst princess ever."

"So what?" Holden said. "Being a princess is lame."

"Lame?" Beautianna repeated. "What do you mean?"

"Well, you have to be prim and proper all the time and say things like, 'Oh, Duchess Duckington, we'd be delighted to have you for tea.' You can't eat a jelly donut or put ketchup on your hamburger because it might stain your billion-dollar dress. And you never get to enjoy parades, because you're always way at the back, waving to everyone."

"Hold on," Maddie said, getting offended. "A princess is the greatest thing you can be. It's magical and elegant and fun. It's every little girl's dream."

"Psst!" Holden said. He leaned in and whispered in Maddie's ear. "Um, I thought you didn't want her to marry the prince. We're trying to talk her out of it, right?"

"Right, right," Maddie said. She couldn't believe any woman would turn down the chance to be a princess, but that's exactly what they needed Beautianna to do.

"Look, lady," Holden said. "Do you love this dude?"

"No, of course not," Beautianna said with a laugh.

"You don't? But I thought he was so handsome and charming?" Maddie said.

"That's what they tell me," Beautianna responded. "I've been so busy sorting through tablecloths and tasting appetizers, I've barely even spoken to him."

"That's messed up," Holden said. "What if this marriage doesn't work out? Do you know what a pain it is to get divorced? My mom cried every night for, like, a year. You should really talk to this guy soon."

"I want to," she said, "but there's procedure to follow. First I need to have a royal guard summon him."

"Holden's a royal guard!" Maddie said.

"Yeah, I'll summon him."

"Really?" Beautianna asked.

"Sure," Holden said, turning toward the doorway. "Just tell me where he hangs out."

"Well, in his throne room, I imagine," Beautianna said.

"Right. And where's that?"

"What? You don't know where the throne room is?"

Maddie forced a laugh. "Oh, of course he does. He's a royal guard." She nudged Holden in the side and winked at him. "He'll bring the prince back as soon as he finds him."

Holden sighed as he left the room. "Don't hold your breath," he said quietly. "It's a big palace."

For the first time ever, Maddie was a little sad to see Holden leave. All his negativity had done wonders to sour Beautianna on being a princess. Maybe his unpleasantness was valuable after all.

No sooner was he gone than Beautianna pulled Maddie toward a chair. Maddie had to wipe broken glass off the cushion before she could sit down. "Sissy, can I tell you a secret?" the wicked stepsister said.

"Of course. We're sisters, right?"

"That wasn't my glass slipper that the prince tried on my foot," Beautianna confessed. "I mean, I don't even like glass. If Mother bought me a shoe like that, I probably would've smashed it."

"So you're not the woman he fell in love with at the ball?"

"No. There must be another woman in this kingdom with the same size foot as me. Can you believe that?"

"I guess so," Maddie admitted. "But why didn't you tell the prince?"

"Mother's making me lie so that he'll marry me. Since I was a little girl, it's been her dream that I'd someday marry a prince."

"Then you need to talk to Mother."

Beautianna gasped, petrified at the thought. "You shouldn't have said that!" Just then, a wicked wind tore through the castle, blowing out every candle and casting the room in an eerie dimness. A long, pointed shadow appeared on the craggy stone wall, and with the sound of thundering footsteps, it drew closer, followed by a voice that sent a chill down Maddie's and Beautianna's spines.

"Did I hear you talking about me?" the deep voice echoed, and into the room stepped the fearsomely pale face of Pernicia V. Rockbotton.

"H-h-h-hello, Mother," Beautianna stammered.

Chapter 8

Holden had no idea how to find a throne room in a castle. Was it near the front? Hidden in the basement? High up in one of the turrets? He walked past a bedroom, a library, and a room that contained nothing but helmets.

No thrones so far.

Then, he turned a corner and found himself staring at the same portrait of Prince Andrew he had passed five minutes earlier. He was going in circles. This was like trying to navigate the corn maze at the Halloween fair, only Holden never had any problem with that, because he just snuck between the corn stalks when he got lost.

Why couldn't there be a directory, he wondered, like at the mall, with a little crown marking the throne room and an arrow saying, "You are here"? Of course, if this were a mall, Holden would've stopped at the food court by now for a slice of pizza. Being a royal foot soldier was making him hungry.

Yeah, never mind the throne room, he thought. He decided to look for the kitchen instead. It sounded easier anyway. After all, he couldn't ask someone where the throne room was, or they'd know he wasn't really a royal foot soldier. No one would expect him to know where the kitchen was, though.

He stopped a noble-looking woman to ask for directions. "Excuse me, can you tell me where the royal kitchen is? I'm royally hungry."

"Yes, of course," the woman said, pointing down the hall. "Down that corridor to the right, two doors past the throne room."

"Yeah!" Holden said. He was so excited to get all that information that he held up his hand for a fist bump. "Hit me!" he said.

"Absolutely not!" the woman huffed.

"C'mon, it's just a fist bump," Holden explained.

"Hmph!" the woman scoffed. She turned her back on him and continued down the hallway.

Now the only decision Holden had to make was where to go first. The fate of Cinderella rested on him going to see the prince as soon as possible. Then again, a slice of pizza sounded really good.

As he approached the throne room, he could hear a violin playing a romantic waltz inside. One more reason to choose the kitchen. He couldn't stand classical music. Peering inside, he saw Prince Andrew dancing across the room with a doll in his arms. Holden didn't know much about dancing, but he had to admit this guy was pretty good.

"You can come in, Charles," the prince said, not even turning around to look at the doorway.

"Excuse me?" Holden said.

The prince stopped dancing and looked at Holden. "It's all right. I've been expecting you, Charles."

"I'm not Charles," Holden said.

"Oh, sorry. Edmond, of course. Come in, Edmond."

"Who's Edmond?" Holden asked.

"You'll have to forgive me," the prince explained. "I'm not very good with faces. What is your name, soldier?"

"I'm Holden, um, sir."

"Sir Holden? Well, you must be one of my higher-ranking guards to have been knighted. I apologize for not recognizing you."

Behind Holden, another soldier appeared. "The princess's crown has arrived, Sire."

Bowing before the prince, the soldier presented a crown on a velvet pillow. The crown was encrusted with jewels and made from solid glass.

"Oh, thank you, Charles."

"I'm Edmond, Sire."

"Oh, drat. Sorry."

Holden couldn't believe it. This prince really was bad with faces. No wonder he couldn't tell that Beautianna wasn't the woman he had met at the ball.

"What do you think, Sir Holden?" Prince Andrew asked, showing him the crown. "Won't my bride love this?"

"Is it made of glass?" Holden asked.

"Yes! Like those magnificent slippers she wore at my ball. I've made everything out of glass. Her crown, her scepter, even her throne." He lifted up a sheet, revealing a throne made entirely of glass.

"Not the best idea," Holden said. "She gets a little smashy."

"Has she broken something?"

"She's broken just about everything, and she ripped her wedding dress — on purpose."

"Is my princess unhappy?" Prince Andrew looked genuinely concerned, even hurt.

"I wouldn't exactly say unhappy."

The prince sighed in relief. "Oh, thank goodness. Her happiness is all I yearn for in life."

"Dude, she's bonkers."

"Bonkers?"

"Wacko, demented, totes *loco*. Buddy, your bride is a major head case, and if I were you, I'd get down there before she burns the whole castle down."

"I cannot see her before the wedding. It is tradition."

"Well, it's a messed-up tradition. You should spend as much time as you can with someone before you marry them. That's why my mom and dad didn't last. So when she met Roger, they took it slowly. He's made her happy, too, even if he did bring his annoying daughter along with him."

"Who's Roger?" the prince asked.

"Never mind," Holden said. "C'mon, you need to talk to your bride. Consider yourself summoned." He grabbed the prince by the arm and led him to the hallway. As soon as they got there, Holden hesitated, looking left, then right, unsure exactly how he found the throne room in the first place. "Um, maybe you should lead the way," he said to Prince Andrew.

Chapter
9

When Maddie was younger, she used to have nightmares about Cinderella's wicked stepmother. She would wake up crying, and her father would come running into her bedroom, assuring her that the wicked stepmother was a character in a story and not someone who could hurt her. Now, though, as this evil villain stood two feet away from her, it was hard for Maddie to believe she was anything less than real, and that made her scarier than ever.

It didn't help that Beautianna was also nervous in their mother's presence. "H-h-h-hello, Mother," she stammered.

Then, Pernicia V. Rockbottom did something Maddie never expected. She reached down and gave her a warm hug. "My dear girls!" she exclaimed, drawing Beautianna into the embrace as well. "To think, by this time tomorrow, we shall all be royalty!" Pernicia let go of the girls and flitted about the room merrily, like a woman half her age. "We'll move into the palace and bid that horrid little cottage goodbye forever." She twirled and giggled with delight. She looked spectacular, too, in a black and gray dress that was covered with diamonds. Maddie had never seen anything so beautiful. It must have cost a fortune.

Maddie summoned up the nerve to speak. "Is that what you're wearing to the wedding?" she asked.

"What? This? Don't be silly! It's just a housedress!" Pernicia replied.

"It's so shiny," Maddie said.

Pernicia winked at her. "Well, if you like it, I can have one made for you."

"You can?"

"My dear, you shall be a duchess. You can have any dress you want."

Maddie's mind began to wander. Her? A duchess? Maybe she didn't need to change this story after all. Maybe she could enjoy this new life for a while. Who wouldn't want to live in a fairy tale, as royalty? It sure beat being in the fifth grade in Middle Grove, New Jersey.

"Looks like we'll have to get you a new dress too," Pernicia said, discovering the rip in Beautianna's sleeve.

"Yes, Mother. I guess so," Beautianna replied.

Maddie sighed. She knew she couldn't stay in this story forever. That would mean Cinderella would stay locked in the dungeon. She even felt sorry for Beautianna, who clearly had no interest in marrying the prince.

"As long as you're making her a dress," Maddie said, "why not make one she actually wants to wear?" Maddie grabbed Beautianna's design from the shelf.

"Sissy, no!" Beautianna protested. She tried to stop Maddie from giving Pernicia the sketch, but it was too late. Pernicia was already looking at it — and laughing.

"Glamoremma, you were always my funny one. As if I'd let my daughter marry the prince in this ridiculous frock!"

"She designed it herself."

"All the more reason not to wear it!" Pernicia scowled. She tossed the design onto the floor and stomped on it as if she were squashing a spider. "A princess toiling as a lowly seamstress. That's a task for your stepsister, Cinderella, if she had any talent. Girls, we are a royal family now, and we need to start acting like it. We must demand only the best, and it shall be provided to us. Massages with imported oils, feasts of the most succulent lamb and caviar, lavish trips to other lands. Just name what you want, and it shall be yours!"

Beautianna took a deep breath. "I want to go to art school!" she exclaimed.

At that moment, any trace of a smile disappeared from Pernicia's face. The room grew dimmer, as if a great storm cloud had formed overhead. A chill fell over the castle, and the wicked stepmother's eyes seemed to glow. This was the face Maddie recognized from her childhood nightmares, the face of pure evil.

"Listen to me, little girls," Pernicia snarled. "You don't seem to appreciate all I've done for you. Since you were born, I've trained you to behave like princesses — to have the best manners and the highest standards of beauty and grace. I've kept Cinderella in rags and fed her scraps so that my girls could have the best and attract a prince's affection. And it worked. Now, at last, my dream has come true. We shall be royalty, the three of us, and you will show your gratitude to me by doing as you are told. There will be no art school and no silly dresses, nothing to suggest that we are anything but regal and entitled to all the riches the kingdom has to offer. Am I understood?"

Beautianna looked to Maddie for help, but Maddie felt like she was back in her nightmares. She wanted to cry and have her dad come hug her, but she knew that wouldn't happen. She found herself unable to say anything.

"Good," Pernicia growled. "I'll have a new wedding dress made up at once." She turned to leave the room, but before she had both feet into the hallway, Beautianna summoned up her courage and shouted back at her.

"What about my dream?" she said.

Pernicia stopped short, slowly turning back into the room. "Your dream?" she asked, calmly.

"I never wanted to be a princess," Beautianna said. "It sounds so horribly boring, Mother! And what if I want to eat a jelly donut? Or put ketchup on my hamburger?"

"What?" Pernicia scolded. "Stop this nonsense, Beautianna. If the prince were to hear you say such a thing, he might not want to marry you."

Instead of quieting down, Beautianna shouted, "Good! I don't want to marry him! I don't love him!"

"Then the wedding is off!" called a voice from the hallway. Maddie, Beautianna, and Pernicia all turned at once, gasping as they spotted the prince standing in the doorway behind them. At his side was Holden, who looked as shocked as anyone else.

"You've broken so many things in this room," Prince Andrew said, "but I'll not allow you to break my heart. Guards, have these women escorted from the castle immediately."

"Your Highness —" Pernicia begged as soldiers marched into the room. "No!"

"Her first!" the prince said, motioning toward Pernicia. "And make sure you take back that ridiculous dress she's wearing. I'm glad you won't be my mother-in-law," Prince Andrew said to Pernicia. "You would've been a royal pain in the rear end!"

He stormed out of the room, as guards grabbed Pernicia, Beautianna, and Maddie. "Holden," Maddie whispered, "what about Cinderella?"

"Oh, right," Holden said. He stepped into the hallway and called out to the prince. "What about their stepsister? Should I have her thrown out too?"

"Yes," the prince declared. "The sooner the better."

Maddie groaned. "I didn't want her thrown out."

"Hey," Holden replied as guards led the women away, "it beats being in the dungeon."

Chapter 10

If there was one good thing about being escorted out of a castle by royal guards, it was that Maddie no longer felt that Holden's picture of her morning hair was the most embarrassing thing that had ever happened to her. Whenever a villain is defeated, good people celebrate, and that's what they were doing as Maddie walked down the long hallway with Pernicia and Beautianna. Members of the royal staff laughed and cheered. Some of them even danced. The maids and butlers who helped Beautianna pick out tableware exchanged elated hugs. Everyone was glad to see these women go and thrilled that they would no longer be marrying into the royal family.

"Boo! Boo!" Pernicia shouted back at the hecklers. "I promise you'll regret this!"

Maddie was mortified, but she also felt sorry for Beautianna. Her mother had trained her to act like a diva, thinking that was how a princess was supposed to behave.

Underneath, though, Maddie now knew Beautianna was a girl like her, with her own feelings and dreams. She didn't want to hurt anyone. She wanted to go to art school. If not for her mother spoiling her all her life, she might've been pretty cool.

As they stepped outside, Maddie saw a royal carriage waiting for them. It was tall and sparkly, with beautiful white horses in front. Despite the fact that she had been led from the castle in shame, Maddie felt a pinch of excitement that she would get to ride in such a majestic fairy tale vehicle.

Pernicia was the first to board the carriage, and the crowd that had gathered applauded wildly as she took a seat on the bench. Scowling at them, Pernicia reached out and slammed the carriage door shut behind her, before Maddie and Beautianna could get in.

"Mother, wait!" Beautianna cried, reaching for the carriage door.

Pernicia swatted her hand away. "Take me away from this miserable place!" she demanded.

The driver looked down at Maddie and Beautianna. "But, ma'am, your daughters," he said.

"I have no daughters!" she thundered, putting her feet up on the opposite bench. "Away!"

With that, the carriage sped off, leaving Maddie and Beautianna behind. Even the staff members who had come to laugh at them were shocked at Pernicia's cruelty toward her own children.

Beautianna began to cry. "I thought Mother loved us, but she just loved the idea of being royalty."

Maddie put her arm around her. "You still have a sister who loves you," she said.

"Thanks, Sissy." Beautianna hugged her back, then together, the two of them began to walk through the palace gates. Maddie knew it wouldn't be an easy trip, but she also knew that Cinderella had done it with one shoe, so one way or another, they would make it home.

Chapter
11

Holden had never been as nervous as he was descending the dark, moldy staircase to the dungeon. Cinderella had been sharing a cell for hours with Darreth, a man so awful that thunder boomed whenever his name was spoken. You have to be pretty nasty if even the weather hates you. As he reached the dungeon, Holden half expected to see Cinderella crushed into a small cube or chopped up into a salad. He was relieved when he heard her crying. At least it meant she was still in one piece.

"I never meant to cause all that disease and hardship!" a deep, blubbering voice wailed. Holden stopped short and held his lantern out toward the cell. It wasn't Cinderella who was crying. It was Darreth.

Darreth was a massive wall of a man — his smallest muscle was twice the size of Holden's entire body. But right now, it was hard to be afraid of him, because he was doubled over in Cinderella's lap, bawling his eyes out.

She gently ran her hands through his hair, like a mother comforting a sad child.

"There, there," Cinderella said. "Let it all out." She noticed Holden approaching and held up her hand, as if to ask him not to interrupt. So Holden stood back and watched, in awe. The most fearsome man in the kingdom had been locked in a cell with this woman for only a few hours, and he now seemed about as harmful as a kitten.

"I can see the good in you, Darreth," Cinderella said. *BOOM!* "Don't listen to that thunder. One day, birds will chirp when they hear your name, and children will sing."

"My stepbrothers were supposed to be the conquerors," Darreth sniffled, wiping his eyes. "That's what she always told them. She said I'd never be good enough to take over anything. I just wanted her to notice me!"

"I know how it is," Cinderella assured him. "I have a stepmother too."

"Now everyone sees me as a bad guy . . . and a failure!"

"We all have our own eyes," Cinderella comforted. "So why use anyone else's? What matters isn't what other people see. What matters is, how do *you* see you?"

"I never thought of it that way," Darreth said.

Darreth raised his head and thought about what Cinderella had said. Holden finally saw an opening for him to interrupt. "Ahem," he said, clearing his throat to get their attention. "Palace guard coming in! If there's anything you don't want me to see you doing, stop doing it now!"

Darreth wiped his eyes and blew his nose in his sleeve. "You can come in," he said.

Holden unlocked the door to their cell. "The prince has ordered for you to be released," he said. "You're free to go."

He swung the door open, but before Cinderella could even stand up, Darreth leapt to his feet, cheering. "Whoopee!" he exulted.

"No, not you," Holden said. "You're still under arrest."

"Oh," Darreth said, sitting down glumly.

"It's okay," Cinderella assured him. "I'll visit you."

"Really?" Darreth asked.

"Of course."

Then Cinderella leaned down and gave the hulking giant a tender kiss on the forehead.

With a creak and a clank, Holden closed the gate to the cell. "Goodbye, Cinderella!" Darreth shouted.

"Farewell, Darreth!" she replied.

Holden shook his head at how weird the whole situation was, and as he led Cinderella upstairs toward the light, the soft rumble of thunder rattled one more time from far off in the distance.

Chapter 12

When most girls dream of being Cinderella, they skip ahead to the part where her fairy godmother dresses her up and sends her off to meet the prince. But Maddie suddenly found herself in the part of the story where the heroine was absolutely miserable, hopelessly scrubbing the floors of the wicked stepmother's house. After she and Beautianna had been thrown out of the castle, Cinderella had joined them for the long walk home, and the trek was pure agony. Miles and miles of dirt roads and muddy fields. But when they finally reached the wicked stepmother's cottage, things got even worse.

They practically collapsed at the doorway, they were so exhausted and hungry. All Maddie wanted was to have a Hot Pocket and go to bed, but when they stepped inside the house, they were greeted instantly by the scowling face of Pernicia V. Rockbotton. She shoved brooms and scrub brushes into their hands and gave them chores to do. For the first time ever, she even ordered her precious daughters to pitch in with the housework. There were no more favorites here. Pernicia's daughters were finally equal to her stepdaughter — equally loathed.

She informed the girls, with her usual cruelty, that they would not be able to have dinner until all the chores were done and the floor was clean enough to eat off.

"But why?" Beautianna had asked.

"Why, because you'll be eating off it!" Pernicia replied with a vicious cackle.

Cinderella got right to work. This was nothing new for her. Maddie was impressed with how well she handled the hardship. She was even humming as she scraped the bristles of her brush back and forth across the hard stone floor. Beautianna wasn't handling it quite as well.

"I just want to eaaaaaaat!" she wailed. "This is agony. I hate chores." Pernicia had instructed her to clean the dirty pots and pans, which were piled up to the ceiling, and Beautianna barely had the strength to begin.

Maddie had the worst chore of all. She was ordered to clean Pernicia's underwear. She sat beside a large washing bucket, dipping them in and out, over and over.

It didn't help that she had to listen to Beautianna whine the whole time.

"I can't do it anymore! I'll never finish!" the once-spoiled stepsister wailed. She threw her washrag on the floor and bent over the counter, weeping.

As shrill and frustrating as Beautianna was, Maddie couldn't help feeling sorry for her. All she had done was break off an engagement to a man she didn't love, and only after Maddie and her brother talked her into it, which made Maddie kind of responsible.

Maddie set the laundry aside and rose from her seat. "I'll help you," she said. Her hands were aching from all the cleaning she'd been doing, but she moved to the sink and worked through the pain to begin scraping pots.

"But you won't be able to eat until the laundry is done," Beautianna said.

"It's okay. I need a break from washing underwear," Maddie replied.

Beautianna sniffled. "Thank you for this, Sissy! You're the best."

"I'll help too," Cinderella added. She brushed herself off and joined Maddie at the sink.

Beautianna was stunned. "But I've always been so mean to you."

"You just seem like you need to eat," Cinderella replied.

Beautianna was speechless. She had always been handed everything she wanted in life by her doting mother, who had been training her to be a princess. Her sisters weren't out to spoil her, though. They were helping her simply because they cared.

Cinderella and Maddie worked well together. Soon, they had finished a pot and set it out to dry. Beautianna quietly picked up her washrag from where she had thrown it and joined her sisters at the sink. At once, they seemed to lock eyes and smile. For Beautianna and Cinderella, it was the first time they could remember when all three sisters got along.

Chapter
13

The prince was majorly bumming Holden out. He was locked in his throne room in the clothes he'd worn to bed, scarfing down figs while his royal orchestra played minor key symphonies at wall-shaking volume. Holden's mom had done nearly the same thing after her divorce, although in her case, she ate Ben & Jerry's and listened to some band called The Smiths.

Any time someone suggested to Prince Andrew that he should go out and meet someone new, he would shout, "No, I'll never get married. Never, ever, ever!"

Oh, the drama!

Holden didn't take it too seriously, because his mom had also sworn she would never get married again. Then, two years later, she met Roger and was happier than ever. The prince would bounce back, too, Holden knew. He just couldn't wait two years for it to happen. This fairy tale world was driving him crazy.

There was nothing good to eat here, no TV, no decent music. If he had to hear one more pluck of a lute string, he'd lose his mind. At least he had his tablet, but there wasn't much he could do with it other than check the *Cinderella* e-book. It's not like he could blast his "Rockin' Jamz" playlist or even tackle a level of *Fudgie the Fox 4* without everyone coming over to see what he was doing.

Every few minutes, the prince would open his door a crack and summon Holden. When Holden arrived, the prince would give him a handwritten note and insist that it be delivered to Beautianna immediately. The next note would usually come before Holden was halfway down the hall. Holden knew better than to deliver these notes anyway. After his mom's breakup, she would get texts every few minutes from his dad. Soon she groaned and deleted them without looking at the screen. Holden imagined that's what Beautianna would do if he actually trudged across the woods to give her one of these notes.

When Prince Andrew handed him the most recent note, he seemed especially upset. "You didn't deliver that last note, did you?" he asked.

"Not yet," Holden replied.

"Thank goodness! Tear that one up, and give her this one instead." The prince pressed a new note into Holden's palm. "Hurry," he added, "before I change my mind."

Holden walked the note around the corner, out of sight, and added it to a stack that contained dozens of others. He had always wondered what was in those texts that his mom got, so he decided to take a look at the letter the prince asked him to destroy. Making sure no one was around, he unfolded it and peeked inside.

"Miss you," it read. Underneath that, the prince had drawn a smiley face. *That's it?! That's what was so urgent for him to deliver, and then a few minutes later, for him to destroy?* he thought. He put the note back in the stack and decided to read the new one instead. Maybe that would help him figure out why this guy was acting so funny.

In its entirety, the note said: "Hi!"

Grown-ups were weird.

Holden once asked his mom why she never responded to those post-breakup texts, and she said it would only encourage his dad. It gave him an idea. If the prince were ever going to get out of his pajamas and look for his true love, he needed some encouragement.

He needed a note. So Holden sat down to write one.

He had to let Prince Andrew know that his true love was still out there, waiting for him. He needed to sound sincere and romantic. And he needed to sound like a woman. He touched a quill to an inkwell and began to write:

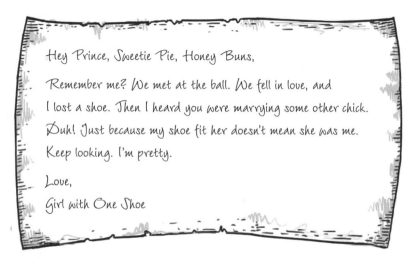

Hey Prince, Sweetie Pie, Honey Buns,

Remember me? We met at the ball. We fell in love, and I lost a shoe. Then I heard you were marrying some other chick. Duh! Just because my shoe fit her doesn't mean she was me. Keep looking. I'm pretty.

Love,
Girl with One Shoe

He folded it up and put it in an envelope, then wrote the word "Prince" on the front. Something about it didn't look right, though. Holden knew he didn't have the neatest handwriting. The prince would never believe this came from a girl. He tried to think about how a girl would write the prince's name. Then he got a great idea. He dotted the "i" in "Prince" with a tiny heart. Perfect.

"But this means Beautianna is not the woman from the ball!" the prince said, aghast, as he read the note. "That would mean that I forgot her face."

"I could totally see you doing that," Holden assured him.

"Forget the face of my true love? But then, did I ever love her at all?"

"Sure," Holden said. "Unless all you fell in love with was her face."

The prince sighed wistfully, thinking back to that magical night. "No, it was more than that. It was the way she danced, the way she smiled, the way she looked at me with her eyes glistening. She was so full of light and joy. I knew she and I could be happy together forever."

"Sounds like you didn't fall in love with her face. You fell in love with her heart."

Prince Andrew nodded. "That's very profound," he said.

"Yeah," Holden added, "you probably would've been into her even if she was a total butt face."

"Absolutely," Prince Andrew agreed, before turning to Holden quizzically. "What's a butt face?"

"Never mind."

Prince Andrew put down the note. "If my true love is still out there, waiting for me, then I must find her!"

"Awesome!" Holden shouted. "But first, I'd change out of those pajamas."

Prince Andrew gazed at himself in the mirror. "Right, good idea," he replied.

Chapter 14

"We did it!" Beautianna cheered, sliding the last clean pot into the cupboard. "I can eat! Finally, I can eat!" She thrust open the pantry doors and ran back and forth, struggling to choose her first treat. "Apples?" she said. "No, pears. Wait, berries! Mmm-mmm."

Maddie wanted to be happy for Beautianna, but she couldn't help feeling annoyed. While Beautianna stuffed her face, Maddie had to go back to cleaning Pernicia's underwear. This wasn't even her real family, and she was working harder here than she ever did at home. Her own stepmother was very nice. Carol would never starve Maddie to punish her, and she'd be mortified to make Maddie hand-wash her underwear. Gross.

She hated to admit it, but the thrill of being in a fairy tale was wearing off. It was fun for a while, meeting Cinderella and being in a castle, but who wanted to experience the part of the story where the heroine was up to her knees in floor grime? Other than the happy ending, Maddie could do without another minute of being in this place.

This was all Holden's fault, and he was still living it up in the palace. It was so unfair.

Then, she felt a hand on her shoulder. "Glamoremma, are you okay?" It was Cinderella. "You seem so upset. Let me help." Cinderella stooped down next to her and picked up a pair of frilly bloomers to wash.

One thing Maddie couldn't argue with was how big Cinderella's heart was. Her two stepsisters had been nothing but cruel to her, but now that they needed help, she was pitching in. Like it or not, Maddie didn't want to leave this fairy tale until Cinderella got the happily ever after she deserved.

As the two of them toiled, Beautianna scooped up as many berries as she could with her two hands. She drew them close to her mouth, ready to shove them in all at once, when she noticed the other two young women still hard at work. For the first time in her life, she felt a nagging tingle in the back of her head. It was a sensation she had never known before — the odd, foreign emotion of guilt. She got the sense that the only way to make it disappear was to stop eating and help.

"Hold on," Beautianna said, sighing. "I'll work too."

"No, please eat," Cinderella assured her. "I'm used to my misery by now."

"Just slide down," Beautianna snapped, setting her stool next to the wash bucket. "Let's get this over with."

Together, the three of them got to work. Maddie soaped the underwear, Beautianna rinsed them, and Cinderella hung them out to dry. The pile of dirty clothes got smaller and smaller. Despite their exhaustion, this chore seemed to go faster than the last one, because their conversation helped them pass the time. They talked about Cinderella's love of animals and Beautianna's art. Maddie had a topic she wanted to bring up, too, and once they were all getting along so well, she saw the perfect chance.

"So, I wonder who the glass slipper really belonged to," she said.

"Well . . . ," Cinderella replied, taking a deep breath.

"Whoever it is, she must be kicking herself," Beautianna interrupted. "I know he wasn't for me, but plenty of girls would've thought that Prince Andrew was a catch. And if she came that close to marrying him, that girl must be utterly heartbroken right now."

"She is," Cinderella said.

Beautianna dropped the pink stockings she was wringing out. "Hold on. Oh my gosh. Was it . . . you?"

Cinderella began to nod sadly, but Beautianna wasn't looking at her. She was looking at Maddie. "Glamoremma, was that your shoe?"

"No, it was mine," Cinderella said.

"Very funny, Cinderella. Where would you have gotten glass slippers? Mother doesn't let you have nice things."

"I guess I can tell you girls. I had some help from my fairy godmother."

"Huh?" Beautianna asked. "What's a fairy godmother?"

"She's a kind older woman with magical powers who watches over you and grants wishes when you need help."

"What?" Beautianna laughed. "You're saying some old fairy lady made you fancy shoes so you could go to the ball? That's preposterous."

"It's true," Cinderella insisted. "She also turned a pumpkin into a coach, mice into horses, and she made me a beautiful blue and white dress."

Beautianna rolled her eyes in disbelief. "Glamoremma, are you hearing this?"

"I think she's telling the truth," Maddie said. "Sure, it sounds a little strange —"

"Strange?" Beautianna repeated. "I think all these chores have made Cinderella positively screwy. Okay, fine. I'll play along. So if you had all these nice things to go to the ball, why did you leave the shoe behind?"

"I was in a rush to get home. The magic wore off at midnight. The coach turned back into a pumpkin, the horses into mice . . . "

"Oh, silly me. I should've known. And you were afraid the prince would lose interest if he saw that your entourage was made up of rodents and vegetables?"

"Exactly."

Beautianna laughed and picked up the pink stockings. "I'll say this, Cinderella. You tell a good story. I'm not saying I believe it, but it's a good story."

Maddie smiled. "It would've been a better story if the prince had tried the slipper on her instead of you."

"Yeah, you'd be married to him right now," Beautianna realized. "Oh well, back to the underwear." She shrugged, and she and Cinderella went back to dunking underwear in and out of the wash bucket.

"We can't give up," Maddie insisted. "Cinderella and the prince were meant to spend their lives with each other. We have to get them back together."

"You would do that for me?" Cinderella said.

"Of course, Cinderella." Maddie realized this was her chance to tell Cinderella something she had always wanted to. "Since I was a little girl, you've been the one who made me believe in true love."

"You've never said anything so nice to me before."

Maddie remembered she was supposed to be a wicked stepsister, but as long as she was changing things in the story, she figured she could change that too. "I'm sorry, Cinderella. I've been very wicked to you, and you don't deserve it. I'll be nicer from now on."

A tear fell down Cinderella's cheek, and she clasped Maddie's hand tightly in her own.

"What do you say, Beautianna?" Maddie asked. "Will you help too?"

Beautianna thought for a moment. "Help Cinderella marry the prince? That would drive Mother nuts." She smiled a devious grin. "Count me in!"

Chapter 15

The prince gathered all of his top advisors for a very important meeting. "It has come to my attention that the woman who broke my heart was not the same woman I fell in love with at the Royal Ball. That woman is somewhere in this kingdom, as heartbroken as I am. I will never be complete without her. If it's the last thing I do, I shall find her!"

Holden smiled, knowing this was the kind of dedication a prince was supposed to exhibit in a fairy tale. Things were finally back on track toward the happily ever after. Better yet, that meant he'd finally be able to get out of this place.

"But how, Your Highness?" one of the advisors asked.

"Well, I have one idea," the prince replied, "but . . ."

"Please, tell us," the men encouraged.

"Okay," the prince said. "We still have the glass slipper. Perhaps we could try it on the other maidens in the village until it slides perfectly onto one of their feet. Then we will know that she is my true love!"

The advisors applauded enthusiastically. They rose to their feet, cheering and shouting out things like, "Good idea!" and, "Brilliant, Your Highness!" and, "Let's begin!"

Holden couldn't believe what he was hearing. He, too, leapt to his feet, shouting, "No! Are you all loony?"

The ruckus quieted down, and every head turned toward Holden. Now the advisors were saying things like, "He disagrees?" and, "He must be mad!" and, "Just what is his problem?"

"That's exactly what you did the last time, and it didn't work. That shoe is going to fit a ton of women!"

The prince nodded, and the advisors began muttering things like, "He has a point" and, "I hadn't thought of that" and, "Well, I feel dumb."

"What do you suggest, then?" the prince asked. "How can I get back to the happiness I felt on that magical night?"

Once again, every eye in the room focused on Holden, and he realized that it was up to him, an eleven-year-old boy, to come up with a plan to save a kingdom, a prince, and an entire fairy tale. "Well, you made a mistake, but you deserve another chance. What if you have a do-over?"

"A do-over?" the prince repeated.

A clamor of confusion rose up. People said things like, "What's a do-over?" and, "Now he's making things up!" and, "It's over, it's done!"

Holden tried to explain. "It's like when I'm playing ball with my buddies, and the ball comes, but I'm not ready, and I miss it. I say, 'Do-over!' and they throw the ball again."

"You want me to throw the ball again?" the prince asked.

"Well, I was talking about baseb —" Holden stopped himself. "I mean, yeah! Throw the ball again! That's your do-over!"

"It's genius! We'll do everything the same. The decorations, the music. We'll ask every woman to wear the same dress she wore that night. I will look out among the crowd and once again, I shall see her. When we dance, I'll know in my heart that she's the one."

A great cheer rose up from the advisors, who circled Holden to pat him on the back for his genius. "I love it!" they said and, "It's sure to work!" and, "Let's get this party started!"

"We'll need a proclamation," the prince said. "The ball shall take place tomorrow night!"

PROCLAMATION!

By order of His Royal
Highness, Prince Andrew,
all unmarried women in the
kingdom are hereby invited
to a Royal Do-Over.

"A do-over?" Maddie said. That didn't sound like royal language to her. She grabbed the scroll from Beautianna and continued to read.

"The prince requests that all guests wear the same gowns they wore to the previous ball, so that he may find the woman he fell in love with that night. This is the woman he intends to make his princess."

Cinderella gasped.

Beautianna gasped.

Maddie grinned. She knew Holden must have come up with this plan to put Cinderella and the prince back together. The little whiner was always begging for do-overs whenever they played a game. Yes, it was definitely him. Her stepbrother had done his part. Now it was her job to get Cinderella to the ball.

"It's a miracle!" Maddie squealed. "Cinderella, you'll have another chance to marry the prince. You still have the dress, right?"

"Yes! It's hidden under my bed!" For the first time in days, Cinderella smiled. Once again, she had hope. She jogged to her room to get her dress, and Maddie and Beautianna held hands and squealed with delight. Their happiness was short-lived, however, because when Cinderella returned, the dress she held had been reduced to rags.

"I forgot," she said. "It didn't look quite as good after I left the ball."

Maddie sighed, remembering how Cinderella's beautiful ball gown had disappeared when the magic wore off at midnight.

Beautianna took the dress from Cinderella and studied it carefully. "I can work with this," she said. "I'll just need a bit more fabric."

"You could make me a new dress?" Cinderella asked.

"Sure," Beautianna said. "I know I haven't been so nice to you. I kind of owe you."

She hugged Cinderella, but once again, there was no time to celebrate. A dark, cold shadow fell over them, which could only mean one thing.

"I have some bad news for you," hissed a voice behind them. "I'm using all the fabric we have to make my own dress."

The three young women turned and saw the vicious face of Pernicia V. Rockbotton scowling down at them.

"You're going to the ball?" Maddie said.

"It said 'all unmarried women,' didn't it? Well, since the unfortunate passing of Cinderella's dear father, I am certainly an unmarried woman." She marched up to Cinderella and snickered at the raggedy dress she was holding. "Cinderella, I see you've found an outfit that perfectly captures who you are. See you at the ball, girls!" With another cackle, she wheeled around and sashayed out of the room.

When Maddie turned to look at Cinderella, she was crying again. "She's right," Cinderella sniffled. "The prince could never love me in these rags."

Maddie and Beautianna locked eyes, both of them unsure how to console Cinderella. Just then, a great wind blew open the shutters of the house, and a giant puff of sparkling smoke swirled into the room. From out of the dust stepped a kind older woman with a warm smile and shimmering silver hair. She waved at Cinderella like she was an old friend. "Yodely-ho, dear!" she sang.

"Oh my goodness!" Cinderella gasped, recognizing her fairy godmother. She stood up to give her a hug, but before she reached her, Beautianna swatted the old lady with a broom. "Aaah! There's an intruder!" she screamed. Before Cinderella or Maddie could stop her, Beautianna was whacking the fairy godmother back and forth across the kitchen. "Mother! Help!"

"What's going on?" Pernicia shouted, thundering back across the cottage toward the kitchen. Her shadow began to fall across the room, and Maddie knew in only seconds, she would be standing right next to the fairy godmother. Thinking fast, Maddie tackled the magical old woman and thrust her into the pantry, slamming the door to keep her inside.

No sooner was the fairy godmother out of sight than Pernicia entered the room.

"What is the commotion in here?" she demanded.

"Mother, you wouldn't believe it, there was a —, a —"

"A mouse!" Maddie said.

"A mouse?!" Pernicia and Beautianna said at the same time, shocked.

"Yes. We got a little scared, but it's gone now."

"Is that why you were screaming, Beautianna?"

Cinderella and Maddie silently pleaded with her to play along. Beautianna nodded. "Y-yes, Mother. It was just a mouse."

"You girls!" Pernicia grunted, then headed back upstairs. "If I have one more interruption, I'll cast you out to sleep in the woods tonight!" The girls waited as the wicked stepmother trounced away.

"So who's in the broom closet?" Beautianna asked. "That was no mouse."

"That's who I was telling you about," Cinderella replied. "My fairy godmother."

Beautianna's jaw dropped. "You're kidding, right?"

Maddie opened the door to the broom closet, and the fairy godmother took one sad step forward. In the commotion, a bag of flour had fallen on her head, and she was dusted from head to toe with it.

"Well, rumple my wings! This is not the kind of welcome I'm used to!" she pouted.

"I'm sorry!" Cinderella said. "Beautianna, Glamoremma, this is my fairy godmother."

"So you're real?" Beautianna asked.

"Didn't you notice my wings?" the fairy godmother chuckled. With a twinkle and a grin, she fluttered her wings, and the flapping quickly dusted her off so she looked fresh and clean again.

Beautianna stared in befuddlement. "And you can really do magic?"

The fairy godmother nodded. "Just ask this porcupine."

"What porcupine?" Beautianna said, looking around.

The fairy godmother waved her finger, and instantly, a porcupine appeared, sitting at the kitchen table. "Hi, ladies," the porcupine said. The fairy godmother waved her finger again, and just as quickly, he disappeared.

"That's amazing!" Beautianna cried. "Why don't I have a fairy godmother?"

"Oh, but you do," the fairy godmother chirped. "Everyone does!"

"So can you help me?" Beautianna asked. "Mother's making me do chores now. She won't let me eat. I want to get out of here and go to art school."

"I'm sorry, dear. My magic wouldn't work for you. I'm only Cinderella's fairy godmother. But keep wishing on a star, and I'm sure yours will show up."

She flicked her finger playfully against Beautianna's nose and gave her a friendly wink.

Beautianna pouted. "It's not fair!"

"Please, fairy godmother! You have to help Cinderella," Maddie said.

"Of course. When I last left you, you were at the ball, dancing up a storm with the prince. So now that you're marrying him, you probably have a hundred things I can help you with. Caterer referrals, honeymoon reservations, winning over the in-laws. What'll it be?"

"Actually . . . ," Cinderella said.

"She's not marrying the prince," Maddie explained.

"What?!" the fairy godmother cried.

"I'm afraid things didn't exactly work out the way they were supposed to," Maddie said.

"How is that possible?" the fairy godmother asked. "Did you wear that knockout dress I conjured for you?"

"Yes," Cinderella replied.

"And ride in that amazing carriage?"

"I did."

"And of course, you were home by midnight," the fairy godmother continued.

Cinderella shuffled her feet, looking down at the floor.

"Weren't you?" the fairy godmother asked. "Oh, Cinderella! You had only one rule to follow!"

"It was such a magical night . . ."

"Yes, I know. Thanks to my magic. Which wore off at midnight!" The fairy godmother pouted.

"I'm sorry," Cinderella said sadly.

Beautianna snorted. "I would've followed my fairy godmother's directions."

Maddie could see that the fairy godmother was a tad miffed, so she stepped in to smooth things over. "It's okay, because the prince is having a Do-Over ball."

"A Do-Over ball?" the fairy godmother repeated.

"Yes!" Maddie exclaimed. "Isn't it a great idea? Now Cinderella gets another chance too. So if you can conjure her a new dress, coach, and horses, this time she'll leave nice and early. Right, Cinderella?"

Cinderella nodded vigorously. "Absolutely. I'll be the first one to depart."

"Oh, I'm afraid that's not how it works, my dear. I used up almost all my fairy dust on the last ball. That's why I told you how important it was to leave promptly."

"Please!" Cinderella begged. "You must be able to do something."

"Well, you are destined to marry the prince. I guess we'll have to try. If it's a Do-Over ball, perhaps I can perform some Do-Over magic. That uses a lot less fairy dust. Do you think you can find that same pumpkin from last time?"

"Yes, I know just where it is!" Cinderella cheered.

"Good start. How about the mice?"

"That won't be quite as easy," Cinderella said.

"We'll help you," Maddie said. "We'll find them."

"Perfect," the fairy godmother responded. "That just leaves the dress."

Cinderella held up the tattered clothes she was left with after her last dress had disappeared. "Here you go!" she chirped hopefully.

The fairy godmother cringed. "Oh no!" she said. "I'm not sure there's enough fairy dust in the kingdom to make that look beautiful again." She rolled her eyes. "Really, Cinderella. You could've left at a quarter to twelve and had plenty of time to get out of the castle! Told the prince you were tired! Midnight is very late for a young lady to stay out anyway!"

"Hold on," Beautianna said. "I can fix it. I'll make it into something fabulous. I just need some fabric."

"But if you change it, it won't be the dress the prince is expecting to see," Maddie said.

"Oh, it won't matter," Beautianna assured her. "When that prince sees our stepsister in the gorgeous gown I'm going to make her, he'll forget all about that blue and white frock she wore last time."

"You think you can make something that nice?" Cinderella asked.

"No problem!" Beautianna insisted. "I already have the perfect design ready to go." She reached on top of the cupboard and pulled down a sheet of paper. Maddie recognized it instantly as the garish peacock-feathered wedding dress Beautianna had wanted to wear. "Can you conjure enough fabric for that?"

"I'll try my best!" the fairy godmother said.

"Well, that dress will definitely get his attention," Maddie said. She watched uncertainly as Beautianna got to work.

The fairy godmother was a nervous wreck. She paced back and forth outside Cinderella's house, muttering to herself and wringing her hands.

Maddie was trying her best to stay calm, but the sun was setting, and Beautianna and Cinderella were still inside working on the dress. There wasn't much time, and the old lady's fidgeting was driving her nuts.

"It'll be okay," Maddie assured her.

"Sure!" the fairy godmother said. "That's what I thought the last time!"

Maddie nodded. She had a point. "Did you get the coach and horses back?"

"Sort of. The pumpkin and the mice weren't exactly what they used to be."

"I'm sure you did great," Maddie said.

The fairy godmother sighed. "Let's just hope this dress is spectacular."

"What's taking them so long?" Maddie asked. She knocked on the door. "Guys, it's getting late!"

There was no response. The fairy godmother groaned. "This family doesn't need magic. It needs a good clock. Hurry, ladies!" She pounded on the door with her fist.

The door creaked open. "It's about time!" the fairy godmother huffed. A long leg stepped out. The first thing both of them noticed was the gorgeous, glowing blue and white dress.

As the door opened further, they saw that the leg didn't belong to Cinderella or to Beautianna either. It was another woman — young, stunningly beautiful, yet eerily familiar.

"Not who you were expecting, is it?" the woman said. Once she opened her mouth and flashed her sinister eyes at Maddie, there was no doubt who this woman was.

"M-M-Mother?" Maddie gasped.

"Surprised to see me?" Pernicia purred.

"You look stunning," Maddie said. "And young!"

"I clean up nicely, don't I?" Pernicia purred.

"B-b-but, how did you . . . ? When did you . . . ?"

Pernicia turned toward the fairy godmother. "This must be Cinderella's fairy godmother."

"You know about her?" Maddie asked.

"But of course! Turns out I have one too!" She looked over her shoulder, as another kind-looking older woman stepped out of the house. Her smile was warmer, and her hair was an even more shimmering shade of silver than the fairy godmother's. As she twirled through the doorway, a cloud of sparkles surrounded her and beautiful music played.

The fairy godmother gasped. "Betty?" she asked.

"Yodely-ho, Louise!" the other fairy godmother sang. "I didn't get a chance to tell you about my new assignment."

"Oh, I see my coach has arrived," Pernicia announced. Maddie and the fairy godmother looked up at the most majestic carriage they had ever seen. It was half the size of the wicked stepmother's entire house, with diamonds along the edges and four mighty steeds at the front. "Better go. Don't want to be late."

As Pernicia stepped into her coach, Maddie ran up to Betty, the other fairy godmother, pleading with her. "Why would you help her? Don't you know she's horrible?"

"A fairy godmother's job isn't to judge. Sometimes, the person you get to work for is a sweetie pie. Sometimes," she looked up at Pernicia and shrugged, "she's a total snotface."

"Snotface?" Maddie repeated. "That's a strange word for a fairy godmother to use."

Before Betty could reply, Pernicia stuck her head out of the coach's window. "Hey, whose fairy godmother are you?" she croaked. "Let's go!"

Betty scrambled into the coach, and Pernicia pushed her down into a seat. "Good luck at the ball, girls," Pernicia called out the window. "If you make it in time."

In a puff of smoke, the carriage rode off down the driveway toward the palace.

"We're in trouble, honey," the fairy godmother said, shaking her head. "Betty's good."

Before Maddie could reply, Beautianna's voice rang out from inside. "All right! We're ready!"

The fairy godmother hid her eyes. "I'm not sure I can look."

"I wish I had more time," Beautianna said, "but I did the best I could. Sisters and fairy godpersons, presenting . . . Cinderella!"

She threw open the front door, and instantly, Maddie's jaw dropped. "It's . . . it's . . . quite a dress."

Cinderella stepped outside, decked out in Beautianna's outrageous dress. It was the loudest, wildest outfit Maddie had ever seen, yet somehow, now that she saw it on Cinderella, it looked amazing. It shimmered, it flowed, it showed off all the best aspects of Cinderella's beauty. Of course, she looked breathtaking in a housedress, but this particular outfit seemed to suit her better than Maddie ever imagined.

"Well, I can't keep up with fashion," the fairy godmother said, "but this is definitely a statement."

"You really are talented," Maddie exulted, patting Beautianna on the back.

"Do I really look good?" Cinderella asked.

"Better than good," Maddie said.

The fairy godmother nodded. "You look like the most beautiful woman in the kingdom. But honey, where are your shoes?"

They all looked down at Cinderella's bare feet. "Well, I only have one glass slipper left," she said. "Do you have any more fairy dust?"

"I'm afraid it's gone," the fairy godmother replied. "But you can't go barefoot. Here, take mine." She kicked off a pair of worn brown shoes and handed them to Cinderella. "They're just a couple of plain brown pumps, but they've always been lucky for me."

Cinderella smiled. "I'm so fortunate to have all of you helping me. It's so nice to learn how many people truly care about me." She reached her arms out and drew Maddie, Beautianna, and the fairy godmother into a warm group hug.

"Oh, I can't wait until Mother sees how you look!" Beautianna giggled.

"That will be sooner than you think," the fairy godmother said, pulling away from Cinderella's embrace.

"What do you mean?"

Maddie took a deep breath. "She just left for the ball."

"What?" Beautianna said.

"She's unmarried," Maddie explained, "and it's for all the unmarried women."

"How did she look?" Cinderella asked.

"To put it mildly, wowza!" the fairy godmother said.

Maddie tried to explain. "It turns out she had her own fairy godmother dress her up."

"Hold on. She has a fairy godmother too? And I don't?" Beautianna exploded. "This is not fair!"

Maddie could see that Beautianna was about to melt down. She nudged the fairy godmother in hopes of changing the subject. "Fairy godmother, call the coach!"

"Oh yes, yes!" the fairy godmother paused. "But I want to warn you. It doesn't look exactly like it used to."

The fairy godmother whistled to summon the horses, and four old gray mares stumbled up the pathway to the house. Two of them tried to go in one direction, two in the other, and only the harness held them all together and kept them moving in a straight line. It didn't help that their coachman was asleep.

"What's wrong with the horses?" Beautianna asked.

"Mice don't live very long, you see, so the ones who drove you to the ball a week ago are in their old age now. They're very regal, just a bit slow and confused."

"And why is the driver asleep?"

"Well, I shouldn't have used a hedgehog so close to winter. I'm afraid he's started hibernating." The fairy godmother leaned in and shouted in the driver's ear. "Wake up! WAKE UP, HEDGEY!"

With a monstrous snort, the driver startled awake.

"Do that every few minutes, and he'll be okay."

Cinderella didn't seem concerned about the driver. She was too busy looking at the coach itself. "Um, what happened to the pumpkin?"

Unlike the stately carriage Cinderella rode in last time, this one was lopsided, low in the front and high in the back. Even odder, there were four triangular windows that had not been there before. Together, they seemed to make a happy face on the side of the coach.

"Since the last ball, some boys from the village had gotten their hands on the pumpkin and decided to make a jack-o-lantern. They did a nice job. It makes a great jack-o-lantern, just not a great coach. Not anymore. And they left it outside, so it started to rot a bit. Then the hedgehog took a few nibbles, which you really can't blame him for, since he was storing up food for the winter . . ."

The women all stared silently at the coach, and the fairy godmother hung her head. "I'm sorry," she said. "I'm the worst fairy godmother."

Maddie and Beautianna shared a concerned look.

"Maybe you can park it outside the palace gates, so the prince never sees it," Beautianna said.

"Or I'll say it's my coach," Maddie added. "We'll tell him you gave yours to some orphans."

"Cinderella, what in the stars are you doing, dear?" the fairy godmother asked.

They looked up and saw her delicately stepping into the rotten pumpkin coach.

"Why, I'm getting in my coach," she said.

"But it's a mess," the fairy godmother whimpered.

"I think it's beautiful," Cinderella replied. "I don't care that it doesn't look like all the other coaches. You worked really hard on it. I'm so lucky to have such great stepsisters and a wonderful fairy godmother."

The fairy godmother smiled at Cinderella, with a twinkle in her eye. In that moment, they could all see what it was about Cinderella that the prince fell in love with.

The fairy godmother ran up and gave Cinderella a kiss on the cheek. "Go get him!" she said. Maddie and Beautianna joined her in the coach, and the fairy godmother backed away to see them off.

"Thank you for all your help!" Cinderella waved.

"Aw, my pleasure, sweetie. Now remember . . . midnight means twelve a.m. sharp. Got it?"

"Got it," Cinderella said, as the coach pulled away.

The fairy godmother ran behind the coach up the driveway. "Don't ruin this chance! These mice might not live to make it to another ball!"

Chapter 18

The Royal Do-Over was turning out to be an even bigger event than the first Royal Ball. Everyone appreciated a second chance. The orchestra had tuned up their instruments. The decorators had made the palace look even more opulent. The royal chef himself was making use of the opportunity to switch up the menu. He was trying out a new dish Holden had taught him, something called "Sloppy Joes."

No one was more excited, though, than the prince himself. All afternoon, he'd been asking Holden questions like "Is my hair okay?" and "How does my posterior look in this cloak?" He was a nervous wreck, much like Holden's mom had been before her first few dates with Roger.

"Remember to play it cool," Holden told him, but before he had finished speaking, Prince Andrew bolted from the room. The royal trumpeters were playing their fanfare, which meant the palace gates were opening to the first carriages that had arrived.

"Oh boy, oh boy, oh boy!" Prince Andrew said, jittery with excitement.

Holden rushed to catch up with him. "Don't get too excited. It's not like she's going to be in the first carriage to come through the —"

"It's her!" Prince Andrew shouted as he reached the palace steps. "She's here!"

Holden couldn't believe his eyes.

The door to the first carriage opened, and out stepped a beautiful foot in a sparkling glass slipper. The leg was clad in the stunning blue and white dress, and the woman's hair was set in gorgeous, flowing rings just like Cinderella's. The prince took a deep breath, his heart soaring, as he approached her.

"Well, hey there, Princey!" the woman shouted.

This was not Cinderella. The more Holden checked her out, the more obvious it was to him. She must've noticed the prince dancing with Cinderella at the last ball and done everything she could to copy her look. She had done a fantastic job too. She had perfectly mimicked everything about Cinderella — except her beautiful face and, perhaps, her manners.

"Go ahead. Plant one on there, Princey!" she said, offering him her hand. The prince had yet to realize this was not the woman who had stolen his heart. *Of course,* Holden thought. *He's terrible with faces.*

"I can't believe we've been reunited!" Prince Andrew gushed. "Every night since we first met, I've dreamt of this moment, my fair beauty."

"Aw, you flatterer," the woman said, punching the prince playfully on his arm. "Call me Gloria!"

Gloria flashed a wide smile, and as beautiful as she may have been, her teeth didn't quite measure up. They were crooked and yellow, and one of the front ones was completely missing.

"Dude," Holden said, "this isn't who you think it is."

"What?! Of course I am," Gloria huffed. "I remember the last ball. We danced, we talked, fireworks went off in my head. Now let's get married, Princey!"

"Well, if you're her," Holden interrupted, "then who is that?"

He pointed the prince's attention toward the next carriage in line. A foot stepped out, and it, too, was wearing a glass slipper. The prince gasped and let Gloria's hand slide out of his. As the woman emerged from her coach, the resemblance became even greater. She, too, wore a dress identical to the one Cinderella wore to the last ball, and her hair was made up precisely the same way.

"It's her!" Prince Andrew shouted.

Gloria pouted as the prince helped the woman out of her coach.

"So nice to see you again, Your Highness," the new woman said.

Gloria stepped up beside the woman and elbowed her forcefully aside. "Sorry, honey," she bellowed, "but I'm the woman Princey's in love with!"

"No, I am!"

"What are you talking about?" a third woman said as she stepped out of her own coach. "I'm the woman the prince wants to marry." She, too, was wearing the same Cinderella dress, but she was definitely not Cinderella.

Holden gazed down the line of waiting coaches. Inside each one was a woman who had made herself look as much as possible like Cinderella.

"I don't understand," Prince Andrew said. "What's going on?"

Holden sighed. "This is going to be a rough night."

"Not for me," purred a deep, raspy voice from behind him.

"Great gracious!" Prince Andrew gasped. Holden turned around to see what had gotten his attention, and there stood a tall, statuesque beauty. Though she was dressed like all the other women, her stunning looks stood out from them all. She confidently strode up to the prince and extended her hand for him to kiss it.

"My Lady," the prince said, bowing down. "It is my pleasure." He looked up into her eyes, and as they stared at each other, he became mesmerized.

Holden noticed something familiar about her, but he couldn't quite figure out who she was. There were only so many possibilities, after all. He only knew a handful of people in this fairy tale. This wasn't Cinderella, and it wasn't one of her wicked stepsisters. Who else could it be?

A line of other women formed behind this mysterious beauty, each of them waiting to be greeted by the prince, but he refused to look at anyone but her. It was as if her eyes had a magnetic pull on his attention and he couldn't break his gaze.

"Um, Your Highness," Holden said. "Some other people want to say hi."

"Not now," Prince Andrew responded. "I think it's time for a dance." He led the woman by the hand into the palace, and finally, Holden figured out who she was.

"Pernicia!" he whispered.

With a sinister grin, Pernicia looked over her shoulder at him as she followed the prince inside.

Holden was worried. Cinderella had better get there soon.

Chapter 19

The ride to the palace was a little bumpier than Maddie had expected. The doddering old mice couldn't agree on a direction to go, and the hedgehog coachman was no help, since he could barely stay awake. They kept taking unplanned detours off the roadway and into the woods, and Maddie wished she had a shoulder harness like on a roller coaster to keep her from constantly flying out of her seat. Beautianna tried to put on makeup, but every time the coach jerked unexpectedly to one side, she would end up with lipstick on her forehead. Cinderella was motion sick, holding her head out the window in case she had to throw up. It wasn't quite as magical as Cinderella's ride to the first ball, but it would have to do.

At last, the palace came into view, and all three women were relieved to see other coaches lining the driveway.

"At least we're not the only ones just getting here," Maddie said.

"Um, Sissy," Beautianna corrected her, "I think those women are leaving."

Sure enough, disappointed women were loading into their carriages, having been rejected by the prince. Then came an even bigger setback.

BONG! BONG!

"Is the clock striking midnight already?" Cinderella fretted. They listened as the chimes rang out eight more times. "Oh no!"

Cinderella braced herself and gazed at the carriage, which she was sure was about to transform back into a rotting pumpkin. Then . . . there was silence. The chimes stopped.

"It's ten o'clock!" Maddie said. "There's plenty of time!"

With renewed optimism, the three women headed for the front door and passed by the line of women waiting for their ride home.

It was then that Cinderella noticed that all of them were in blue and white dresses. "Why are all the women dressed the same?"

"I think so they'll look like you," Maddie said.

"And they do!" Beautianna added. "Everyone looks like you . . . except you!"

Cinderella walked on, a little hesitantly, as the ladies at the front door began to notice her and the eye-catching dress Beautianna had made for her.

"What kind of dress is that?" said one woman.

"Didn't you notice the woman he danced with at the last ball?" another woman asked. "If you want the prince to notice you, you should've tried to look a little bit like her." Several of the women laughed mockingly at Cinderella, and she hung her head.

Upstairs on a balcony, Holden heard the commotion and looked down to see what was going on. When he saw Maddie, he breathed a sigh of relief. "Geez, what took you so long?" he yelled down to her.

"Holden?" she called up to him. "Sorry we're late!"

"Just get up here! I'll have to squeeze you into the dance line." Holden went back inside, and Maddie and Beautianna rushed up the steps. When they got to the top, though, Maddie realized that Cinderella was no longer with them.

"Come on!" Maddie said. "It's super late!"

Cinderella softly shook her head. "What am I doing here?" she asked. "They're right. I look all wrong. I'm so nervous I can barely speak. I should go home."

"You go right inside, dear," said a voice. Cinderella turned to see a tall redheaded woman smiling fondly at her. She was warm and sophisticated, and she was the only other woman not wearing a copy of Cinderella's dress. Instead, she had on a stylish black ball gown, which she wore with poise and grace. "A true lady never shows up to a ball in some knockoff dress. Something tells me the prince is going to love what you're wearing. I certainly do."

"Thanks," Cinderella replied. "My sister designed it." She put her arm around Beautianna and smiled proudly.

"Well, your sister is very talented," said the redhead.

With renewed confidence, Cinderella marched up the palace steps, ready to meet the prince. Along the way, she passed by a snickering woman who muttered under her breath, "Too bad the prince is looking for a woman in blue and white."

Cinderella stopped walking and turned toward the nasty woman. "Well, if the prince doesn't like my outfit," she said, "then I don't want to marry him anyway. Come on, sisters!" Cinderella wheeled around and marched toward the ballroom, leaving the catty women speechless. Maddie and Beautianna had to scurry to catch up to her.

"Thanks for sticking up for me, Cinderella," Beautianna said, adding, "You sure are fun to be with!"

Chapter 20

Holden couldn't believe how girly the prince's ball was. The decorations were girly — all flowers and sashes and berry sprigs. The music was girly — no songs where anyone would possibly want to put their hands in the air. But the girliest thing about this bash, of course, was all the girls. Every guest was female, and each one wore tons of makeup, hoping to catch the prince's eye.

What a lame party, Holden thought. *Who would want to go to a party with no dudes?* Who was the prince supposed to talk with about guy stuff, like sports and how weird girls were? Those were not topics that would go over well with this crowd.

At least it gave Holden a view of what all-girl parties were like. He'd always wondered about them. Sometimes on Monday morning he'd hear the girls at school talking about parties they went to over the weekend, like Haley's craft party or Ashley's sleepover. They always sounded so lame, though. Surely when girls got together they did more than talk, right?

Nope.

From what he could see, that's all that was going on here, with the number-two most popular activity being shooting nasty glares at the one woman who got to dance with the prince. Of course, that woman was Pernicia, and she and the prince seemed positively entranced. Even as they strutted and pranced around the ballroom, they never took their eyes off each other. It made him very nervous. Holden had seen that look on his mom's and Roger's faces when they sat together on the couch watching TV.

"How long has he been dancing with her?" Holden asked a woman nearby.

"Too long," the woman said, sighing.

"Yes," said her friend, "he's clearly found who he was looking for." She turned to Holden. "Would *you* like to dance?"

"Me?" Holden said. He looked at the woman, and she started smiling at him the way the prince was smiling at Pernicia. "No way!" He backed away as fast as he could.

Holden knew Cinderella would arrive at any moment, so he had to break up Pernicia and Prince Andrew, fast. He pushed his way through the crowd of women, as word spread among them that there was another man in the ballroom. Some of them waved to Holden. Some whispered things to their friends, then giggled. One blew him a kiss and said, "Hi, handsome!"

Holden was shaking nervously. He'd never received this much attention from girls before. He didn't know how to respond. He just wanted to talk to the prince and get out of this place as fast as he could, before someone kissed him or something. Yikes.

When he reached the dance floor, Holden tried to get the prince's attention, but nothing he did could make the prince look away from the wicked stepmother's eyes.

"Your Highness?" Holden said. "Hello!" He tapped the prince's shoulder. He tugged at his arm. Nothing worked. It was as if the prince were in a trance, unable to break free.

"Would you leave us alone?" Pernicia snapped, annoyed at the intrusion. She turned away from Prince Andrew and shot a vicious glare at Holden. It was a terrifying gaze, so much so that he shrank away from her in fear.

"Sir Holden?" The prince rubbed his eyes and turned toward him. "Were you talking to me?"

Holden realized it was Pernicia's gaze that was keeping Prince Andrew under her spell. Only when she looked away was the prince able to break free.

"Prince!" Holden shouted. He grabbed the prince by the hands and wheeled him around so his back was to Pernicia, breaking their eye contact. "I was thinking maybe you should dance with someone new."

"Well, of course, Sir Holden," the prince said. He looked down at Holden's hands, clutching his so tightly. He shrugged modestly. "Why, I'd be honored."

Thinking that Holden had asked him to dance, Prince Andrew began to twirl him across the ballroom. He didn't notice the panicked look on Holden's face.

Maddie, however, did notice the panicked look on her stepbrother's face, and she thought it was absolutely hilarious. When she entered the ballroom, she had fully expected to see Prince Andrew dancing with someone. She just never guessed that person would be the boy who always swore, "Dancing is the super lamest thing there is!" Yet, there he was, waltzing with the prince as every woman in the kingdom watched. Holden was saying something, over and over, but from where she stood, she couldn't tell what it was.

"Stop! Stop!" Holden protested. "I didn't want to dance with you! Dancing is the super lamest thing there is!"

"Sir Holden," the prince responded. He was no longer looking in Holden's direction. "You must tell me. Who is that stunning beauty?"

Holden turned in the direction the prince was looking, over by the doorway. There were so many women in the way, but finally, through the crowd, Holden saw who the prince was looking at.

It was Maddie.

"Ew! Her?" he asked. He looked back at the prince, then back toward the door. Now he realized the prince was actually staring at the woman next to Maddie. "Oh, you mean Cinderella, right?"

"Cinderella," the prince whispered, stepping toward her. "That's the most beautiful name, for the most beautiful woman I've ever seen."

Cinderella seemed just as pleased to lay eyes on the prince. They were doing that smile thing again.

"Is the prince looking at me?" Cinderella asked. She clutched the hands of her stepsisters in disbelief, feeling once again as if she were living her wildest dream.

"They're all looking at you," Beautianna replied. "Everyone in this entire ballroom is looking at you."

Sure enough, every eye in the room was on the exquisite young beauty in the peacock-feathered dress. No one was more captivated, though, than the prince himself. He slowly walked toward her across the dance floor.

Maddie gave Holden a thumbs-up. She couldn't believe he'd actually done it. Her creepy stepbrother had gotten the prince to notice Cinderella. Maybe he wasn't so terrible after all. Now all they had to do was stand back and watch the moment when true love sparked, then the happily ever after would be restored and she and her stepbrother could go back home. As the prince drew nearer to Cinderella, he held his arms out, and she reached hers toward his. Maddie knew that the moment they touched and began to dance, they'd remember how they felt on that perfect night when they met. She couldn't believe she would be there to witness it. The ultimate fairy tale moment was about to happen two feet away from her.

"Excuse me. I believe we were in the middle of something." Before the prince's hands touched Cinderella's, Pernicia stepped between them, breaking them apart.

"What?" the prince said, shocked. "How dare y —" As he looked into Pernicia's eyes, though, his anger faded and he became hypnotized once again. "How dare you steal my heart the way you have!" he said, taking Pernicia's hands.

"I knew you wouldn't want to dance with that simple peasant girl," Pernicia tutted.

The prince stared directly into Pernicia's eyes, no longer able to look away. "Of course not, my love," he said. "You're the only woman for me."

With a wicked grin, Pernicia led the prince back to the dance floor.

Beautianna stared in awe at the sinister woman who stole the prince away from Cinderella.

"Who is that?" she asked.

Cinderella recognized her easily. "Stepmother," she whispered, feebly, her voice shaking. A tear fell down her cheek. "I can't win," she said, heartbroken as her wicked stepmother whisked away the man she loved.

"Cinderella, you know his feelings aren't real," Maddie pleaded. "She's using magic to win him over."

"That's what I did, though," Cinderella said. "I had my fairy godmother dress me up and make me perfect, and that's who he fell in love with. That woman at the ball wasn't me. I was as fake as she is."

Maddie had never thought about this before. It seemed so romantic when the prince fell in love with Cinderella in the book, but what did it mean? If you use magic to change everything about yourself, then a prince will fall in love with you? Was that the moral of her favorite story?

Cinderella took a step back, then another.

"Cinderella, wait!" Maddie reached out for her, but Cinderella ran from the room as fast as she could.

Pernicia looked at the door as she left and began to cackle softly. For a moment, she broke her gaze with the prince, and he also saw Cinderella running away. As the door closed behind her, he looked at the floor and saw something she had left behind.

A single, ordinary brown shoe.

Chapter
21

After an hour of searching the palace grounds, Maddie and Holden could only be sure of one thing — Cinderella was very good at hiding. It was almost midnight, and the clock was counting down fast, but there was no sign of her.

"You have any luck?" Holden asked.

Maddie shook her head. They sat down, exhausted.

"It's not right," Holden said. "He's going to marry that awful woman instead of someone really nice who deserves it."

Maddie smiled at her stepbrother. "Thanks," she said.

"For what?"

"For finally understanding the story and for trying to fix it. I guess you're not the worst stepbrother in the world."

"I just want to get out of here," Holden groaned, "I want to get back to pro wrestling and good music and video games."

"Hey!" she exclaimed. "That reminds me. Have you checked the e-book? Maybe there's a picture of where Cinderella is."

"Whoa!" Holden said. "That's a good idea. I guess you're not the worst stepsister in the world, either." He pulled the tablet from his coat and opened *Cinderella*. All that was there, though, was a picture of Maddie and him on the palace steps.

"Darn, it's just us," he said.

"Wait." Maddie pointed at the picture. "Who's that behind us?"

"Searching is so hard on my feet!" came a voice from behind them. It was then that they recognized the woman in the picture as Beautianna. Holden quickly fumbled with the power button and tucked the tablet back in his coat before she could see it.

"Did you find her?" Beautianna asked them.

Holden and Maddie shook their heads.

"Well, she couldn't have gone far," Beautianna said. "Not with only one shoe."

"That's what happened at the last ball," Holden said. "She lost her glass slipper, but she got all the way home."

"Really?" Beautianna asked. "I can't believe no one ever told me. It makes such a good story."

"Yeah, it's okay," Holden agreed.

At this hour, the line of women leaving the ball stretched well across the yard. One by one, they climbed into their carriages and headed home.

"We have to find Cinderella before the ball ends," Maddie said. "This could be her last chance to win the prince's heart."

"Yes, or he'll end up with our mother," Beautianna groaned. "I feel like this can't get any worse."

BOOM! From out of nowhere, a clap of thunder shook the sky. "Oh no!" Maddie said. "If it rains, Cinderella will get soaked!"

Beautianna looked up, puzzled. "That's weird. There isn't a cloud in the sky."

BOOM! Another clap of thunder rattled the ground.

"So where's that thunder coming from?" Maddie asked.

Suddenly Holden sprung to his feet. "Guys," he announced. "I think I know where Cinderella is."

In the chilled, musty dungeon, a deep voice echoed through the darkness. "Of course you lost your confidence. That's exactly what your stepmother wanted."

Cinderella sat on the floor outside a dim, squalid cell. She had squeezed her head through the bars so she could rest it on Darreth's shoulder. "My whole life, she's told me I'm not worthy of marrying a prince."

Darreth tenderly wiped away her tears with the cleanest spot he could find on his grungy sleeve. He no longer seemed like a heartless ogre as he tried to cheer Cinderella up. "You have your own eyes, don't you? So why use hers? The question is, how do *you* see you, Cinderella?"

"Darreth," Cinderella replied. *BOOM!* "You're so wise."

Suddenly the door to the dungeon flew open, and in rushed Holden, Maddie, and Beautianna.

"Cinderella!" Maddie shouted.

The dungeon master stepped out and blocked them from going any further. "Hold on! They're having a breakthrough!" He sniffled, clearly moved by Cinderella and Darreth's conversation.

"It's okay," Cinderella said, rising to hug Maddie. "I'm sorry I ran off. I was so upset at seeing Stepmother."

Holden motioned toward the door. "Guys, we have to hurry. The ball won't last much longer. We have to get Cinderella to dance with Prince Andrew."

"But I can't!" Cinderella said. "I don't want to win the prince with magic. It's not right."

"Then show him the real you," Maddie said, stepping forward. She looked at Holden. "Believe me, the real you is better than anyone you can pretend to be."

Beautianna nodded. "It took me a while to see you for who you are, Cinderella. But there's no one in this kingdom more deserving of being a princess than you." She gave Cinderella a tight hug.

Sniffling, Darreth wiped away a tear. "This is so beautiful," he gushed. "Good luck, Cinderella!"

Holding Maddie and Beautianna's hands, Cinderella began to ascend the steps of the dungeon. "Farewell, Darreth," she said, blowing a kiss over her shoulder. As the door swung shut behind her, the faint sound of thunder could be heard from off in the distance.

"I wish you could stay later." The prince stared lovingly into the eyes of Pernicia V. Rockbotton on the palace steps.

"What kind of girl do you think I am?" Pernicia teased. "It's almost midnight!"

"Very well, but before you go, I have one question I must ask you. Was it you that night? At the last ball?"

Pernicia chuckled playfully and batted her eyelashes. "What do you think?"

"Your Highness! Your Highness!" Pernicia and Prince Andrew looked over as Holden ran up to them, out of breath.

"Sir Holden, please. I'm having a special moment with the woman I've proposed to."

"Proposed? No, not her! You're supposed to marry *her*." He motioned toward the doorway, as Cinderella stepped into view.

"Her?" Pernicia cackled. "Ha!"

Cinderella's confidence began to slip away. She hung her head and took a step backward.

In the driveway, Pernicia's coach pulled up, and she took a step toward it. "Would you please help me into my carriage, Your Highness?"

"Of course," Prince Andrew said, raising her up the step to the buggy.

BONG! Pernicia tensed up as the palace chimes sounded. "That's my cue to go," she said, slamming the coach door. The prince stepped back to watch as the carriage pulled away.

BONG! "Enjoy the rest of your evening!" Pernicia hissed out the window at Cinderella. "What's left of it." *BONG!*

"It's almost midnight," Beautianna said. *BONG!* "Cinderella, you should go too." *BONG!*

Cinderella shook her head. "No."

"No?" *BONG!*

"I'm ready to face the prince as who I truly am." *BONG!*

"Mush, driver, mush!" Pernicia shouted, eager to get past the palace gates before the final chime sounded. *BONG!*

"Great idea," Holden said. "You're not the only one who should do that." *BONG!* "Hey, guards! Close the palace gates!" *BONG!*

Before Pernicia could escape, the palace gates slammed shut in front of her. "What's going on?" Prince Andrew asked. *BONG!*

"Watch," Holden assured him. At that moment, the twelfth chime rang out. *BONG!*

The prince turned to Cinderella, as a sparkly cloud encircled her. She didn't move or attempt to hide, and when the cloud faded away, there she was. All the fabric that had been conjured with magic disappeared, and she was back in her tattered work clothes. She had no more makeup, and her hair fell straight down her back. She stood humbly before the prince, looking much as she had while scrubbing her stepmother's floors.

"This is who I am," Cinderella said. "I'm not who I made you think I was. I'm just a lowly peasant girl who scrubs floors day and night."

The prince couldn't take his eyes off her. "You're . . . you're . . . " He struggled for the words.

"I'm Cinderella," she said.

"You're more beautiful than ever," the prince replied. Her flashy clothes gone, Cinderella's inner beauty shone through. Her smile was genuine and warm. Her eyes were the eyes of a caring soul. She did not look perfect, but she was something better than perfect. She was real.

Maddie felt a surge of joy ten times stronger than the *Cinderella* story had ever given her before. This was what true love looked like, she realized. Two people baring their souls and not being able to take their eyes off each other.

Even Holden thought it was kind of sweet.

"Don't forget about our wedding plans!" Pernicia cooed. She stared into the prince's eyes, trying to weave her magic spell over him again. But when he turned to look at her, he saw that she had transformed back to her true self too. For her, that meant that she aged twenty years, and all the lines of cruelty returned to her face. Her coach was now an eggplant, and her mighty steeds were nothing but three cockroaches and a worm. Her magic no longer had any effect on him.

"I'm sorry," the prince said, "I think our wedding is off."

Pernicia shook her fist at the love-struck couple. "She's a peasant girl!" she shrieked. "A common laborer! She sweeps my floors!"

"Not anymore, she doesn't," the prince said, smiling. He turned back to Cinderella and held her hands.

"I should be leaving," Cinderella told him.

"Hold on," the prince replied. "If you don't mind, I have something I'd like to give you first." He pulled out the shoe she had left in the ballroom and placed it in her hands.

"Oh yes," Cinderella said. "I'll need this to walk home."

"No," the prince responded. "You'll need it to dance." He offered her his arm, and a single tear slid down her cheek.

Maddie got choked up, too, because Cinderella and the prince were experiencing something so magical, it never even happened in fairy tales. The loving couple had been given the rare opportunity to feel the overwhelming joy that comes at the onset of true love . . . for a second time.

As the prince whisked Cinderella back inside the castle, Pernicia stood up and began to walk home. "I'm going to find that fairy godmother and murder her," she groaned.

As they watched Cinderella and her prince glide toward the ballroom, Maddie and Holden turned toward each other. "What do you think of the story now?" Maddie asked him.

"Eh," he said. "It'll never be as good as *Star Wars*."

"Well, *Star Wars* never made you cry," Maddie replied. She pointed to a tear that was forming in the corner of Holden's eye.

"Shut up," he said, wiping it away.

Chapter
22

The next day, Cinderella and Prince Andrew were married. The bride wore a gorgeous white wedding dress, so pure it glowed, with a train that stretched as far as the eye could see. No matter where someone stood in its presence, it appeared to glisten, and it was not clear whether the shimmering came from the fabric or the majesty of the woman wearing it. Beautianna had perfectly captured her sister's elegant style in one flawless gown, and everyone agreed it was her greatest design yet.

The ceremony was everything a royal wedding was supposed to be — grand, opulent, and, most of all, swooningly romantic. It was witnessed by everyone in the kingdom. All of them, from the richest aristocrat to the poorest peasant, danced and dined as one. Among them, a most unlikely individual proved to be the life of the party. Darreth, freed from the dungeon at Cinderella's request, was so happy to get a fresh start that he waltzed and tangoed the night away.

The prince, grateful that Darreth brought him together with Cinderella, forgave him for the disease and hardship he had caused and even knighted him. The prince announced that Darreth's new title would be Darreth, Duke of the Dance Floor. When he spoke it aloud, it was greeted not by thunder but by the sound of birds chirping in delight.

The only loyal subject not present was Pernicia V. Rockbotton, who merely heard the cheers of joy from deep in her cell in the castle dungeon.

There were two other people in attendance, too, a boy and a girl who were visiting from the suburbs of New Jersey.

At the ceremony, it was announced that Cinderella's stepsisters would be given royal titles as well, and from now on, they too would be known as princesses. Upon learning the news, all Beautianna could say was, "I'm so happy for you, Sissy!"

"Me?" Maddie asked.

"Actually, I meant Cinderella," Beautianna replied. "My other sister."

The wedding was followed by the biggest celebration the kingdom had ever known, with a magnificent feast, beautiful music, and dancing on into the night. Everyone was overjoyed for the royal couple, even the women who had been jealous of Cinderella, for that is the effect true love has on people. When they see it, every other care in the world fades away and they're reminded of the enchantment and splendor of life and how glad they are to be living it.

"Glamoremma! Glamoremma!" Beautianna rushed up to Maddie. "She loves the dress I made for Cinderella even more than the last one!"

"Who loves it?"

A woman stepped up from behind Beautianna. It was the redheaded woman from the ball, who once again stood out from the crowd in a stylish red cocktail dress. "Your sister is a remarkable designer," she said.

"I know, and I'm so proud of her."

"Do you know who this is?" Beautianna asked. Maddie shook her head.

The woman held out her hand. "My name is Evelyn Thurndorm. I'm the dean of the Royal Academy of Design. I've offered your sister a position in our upcoming class."

"You're going to art school?" Maddie asked her.

"Eeeeeeee!" Beautianna squealed with delight.

"We'll see you on campus," Ms. Thurndorm said, excusing herself.

"Oh, Beautianna, this is awesome!" Maddie cheered. "I'm so happy for you." She gave Beautianna a warm hug.

As they separated, Beautianna eyed her suspiciously. "You're not really her, are you?"

"What?" Maddie said.

"My sister, Glamoremma. That's not who you are."

Maddie fidgeted nervously. She had tried her best to be part of the story. Had Beautianna figured out that she was an eleven-year-old girl trapped in Glamoremma's body?

"Why would you say that?"

"I noticed it when I almost hit you in the head with the goblet and you didn't strangle me. There was something different about you."

"I'm sorry, Beautianna."

"Don't be sorry! You got me out of marrying a man I didn't love. You helped me believe in myself. Now my dream is coming true. It's so obvious to me now. You're my fairy godmother!"

Beautianna grabbed Maddie in a tight embrace. Maddie was speechless.

Just then, Holden snuck up behind Beautianna and tapped Maddie on the arm. Then he showed Maddie the screen of his tablet. "We got it," he whispered.

"Got it?" Maddie asked. She peered over Beautianna's shoulder and saw the words as Holden read them. "And they all lived happily ever —"

Before Holden could say the last word, he and Maddie felt a magical force drawing them back through the screen of their tablet and out of the fairy tale world.

Chapter
23

"— after," Holden finished. When he looked up from his tablet, he saw that he was back in his bedroom, in his old body and his pajamas. Maddie stood next to him, staring at her diorama, which had changed again. Now it displayed Cinderella's wedding day, with her two stepsisters smiling proudly at her side.

"I guess we really changed it," Holden said. "Because of you and me, *Cinderella* is different now. How about that?"

"You know, fairy tales change all the time," Maddie replied. "The Grimm brothers wrote a version of *Cinderella* where the wicked stepsisters cut off parts of their feet to make them fit in the glass slipper."

"Whoa, that's sick!" Holden said. "We should've tried it."

"Well, I like it the way we made it," Maddie told him. "I never would've guessed it, but we made a good story together, you and me."

"So you admit I was right? *Cinderella* was not a good story."

"It was a great story!" Maddie said. "It just . . . needed a little fixing."

They looked at the clock. "Whoa, we should go to sleep," Holden said.

"Yeah," Maddie replied. She thought about giving Holden a hug, but she settled for a smile instead. And he smiled back. She picked up her diorama and headed for the door.

"Good night," she told him.

"Good night, sis," Holden replied, yawning.

They were both very happy to get to bed at last. It was way past midnight.

THE END

About the Author

Jerry Mahoney loves books — reading them, writing them, and especially ruining them. He has written for and ruined television shows, newspapers, magazines, and the Internet. He is excited to finally be ruining something as beloved as a fairy tale. He lives in Los Angeles with his husband, Drew, and their very silly children.

About the Illustrator

Aleksei Bitskoff is an Estonian-born British illustrator. He earned a master's degree in illustration from Camberwell College of Arts in London. In 2012 he was a finalist for the Children's Choice Book Award. Aleksei lives in London with his wife and their young son.

Glossary

depict (di-PIKT)—to show or describe

diorama (dy-uh-RA-muh)—a model representing a scene with three-dimensional figures, often in miniature

eerie (EER-ee)—strange and frightening

infuriate (in-FYUR-ee-ate)—to make someone very angry

majestic (muh-JESS-tik)—very impressive or behaving in a dignified way, as a king or queen might do

mortified (MOR-tuh-fyed)—extremely embarrassed

opulent (OP-yuh-lent)—costly and luxurious

ornate (or-NAYT)—elaborately or excessively decorated

preposterous (pri-PAH-stur-uhs)—completely absurd

toil (toil)—to work hard for a long time

tradition (truh-DISH-uhn)— a custom, idea, or belief passed down through time

triumph (TRY-uhmf)—to win or succeed

turret (TUR-it)—a small tower on a building

vile (VILE)—extremely unpleasant

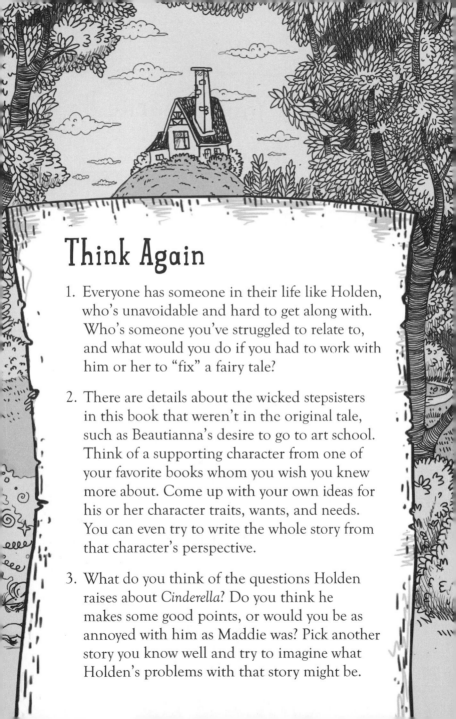

Think Again

1. Everyone has someone in their life like Holden, who's unavoidable and hard to get along with. Who's someone you've struggled to relate to, and what would you do if you had to work with him or her to "fix" a fairy tale?

2. There are details about the wicked stepsisters in this book that weren't in the original tale, such as Beautianna's desire to go to art school. Think of a supporting character from one of your favorite books whom you wish you knew more about. Come up with your own ideas for his or her character traits, wants, and needs. You can even try to write the whole story from that character's perspective.

3. What do you think of the questions Holden raises about *Cinderella*? Do you think he makes some good points, or would you be as annoyed with him as Maddie was? Pick another story you know well and try to imagine what Holden's problems with that story might be.

Want to Ruin Your Favorite Book? Here's How!

Did you know the story of *Cinderella* has been around for hundreds of years? Most people credit the French writer Charles Perrault with writing the version we know today. He published his version way back in 1697. Other versions have appeared in China, Indonesia, Iran, and dozens of other countries. The Brothers Grimm even wrote a version in which the wicked stepsisters cut off parts of their feet to try to fit into the glass slipper. Yuck!

One of the things that makes *Cinderella* such a great story is that different writers can put their own spin on it, and the story still holds up. This book was my opportunity to rewrite *Cinderella* the way I wanted to, and I had lots of fun doing it. I didn't understand how the prince could fall in love with a woman one night and then have no memory of what she looked like afterward. So I played around with that idea and made it a running joke: the prince has face blindness!

You can do the same thing — with *Cinderella*, or with any story.

First, read it a few times. The first time you read any story, don't look for flaws or things you want to change. Just enjoy it and let the author take you on his or her journey. The more you reread it, though, the more certain details will stand out to you. They might be logic problems, character inconsistencies, or just choices you wouldn't have made if you'd been the writer.

Now, you're ready to do your version. Think of what changes you wish you could make. They can be little ones that just change a scene or two or gigantic ones that flip the whole story on its head. Then make them! Turn a sad ending into a happy one. Make yourself the main character and explore how you would've acted differently. Tell the whole story with dogs, or in Colonial times, or in outer space! The only limit is your imagination.

The most important thing, though, is to choose a story that you love. Because here's the secret: if you truly love a story, you'll never actually ruin it. By finding a new way to tell it, you'll just make your readers appreciate the original even more, and you'll give them something new to enjoy at the same time.

Happy writing!

Jerry

FIND MORE MAGICAL
STORIES AT
WWW.MYCAPSTONE.COM

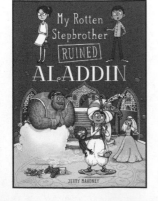

My Rotten
Stepbrother
RUINED
ALADDIN

JERRY MAHONEY

My Rotten
Stepbrother
RUINED
BEAUTY AND THE BEAST

JERRY MAHONEY

My Rotten
Stepbrother
RUINED
SNOW WHITE

JERRY MAHONEY